SUPERHERO CITY
-GHOUL-

by
Eddie Skelson

PANDEMIC PRESS

Heroes may not be braver than anyone else.
They're just braver 5 minutes longer.

Ronald Reagan

Prologue

Excerpt of Speech, Three times President, Donald Drumpf 2023

...The threat posed by people who have these so-called super powers, or Enhanced individuals as they are being labelled, cannot, I repeat CAN... NOT be underestimated. That is why I have issued an executive order requiring all persons in possession of powers and abilities beyond the scope of normal people to register their details with our new agency, the Enhanced Persons Monitoring Division. Anyone who fails to register, or parent or guardian of a child under the age of eighteen showing abilities, will be considered an enemy of the state.

Folks, all we want to do is ensure the safety of us all, including the Enhanced. The last thing we want is a repeat of the Bowling Green Massacre, am I right? Trust me, I know super powers, no one knows super powers and super heroes like I do. But it's not just heroes out there, its villains, criminals, thieves and rapists that a bullet can't stop. Imagine that. They are out there right now and you don't know who they are. You don't! So let us take care of all that.

Enhanced individuals, we will make sure that you are treated fairly and with dignity. We have friends in many corporations and of course our fantastic military, who can help you find gainful employment.

You know a lot of people ask me if I have super powers and I just say, folks, I'm the most popular President in history according to all of the polls, you can check them, it's true. I think that's super enough, don't you?

Thank you and God Bless America.

Biohazard Quarantine and Containment Facility, Arizona, very, very deep underground

'Do we know what it is yet?' Commander Hank Carver asked. His eyes didn't leave the wall of supra-reinforced glass giving him a one-way view into the spacious holding chamber before him.

'We know what it isn't,' Professor Wulf Nils replied. 'It's not an Enhanced. It's not even human.'

The professor stood just behind the Commander, choosing to keep the substantial frame of Carver between him and the creature, regardless of the security measures in place.

'How is that possible?' Carver said, quietly.

It certainly *looked* human to him, at least most of the time. Sometimes it appeared to warp a little, as though it were a recording that had lagged or stuttered and he experienced something similar before. They had an Enhanced on their payroll who *projected* herself. She could produce an incredibly realistic clone, a mirror image, conjured from light via some mutation they had yet to reverse engineer. When she weakened from maintaining the illusion, she could only sustain the facsimile for about ten to fifteen minutes, the projection would *glitch* as her control over the light particles producing it loosened.

The creature did this, it *glitched* every now and then, a sudden ripple or warp in its appearance. But Carver was certain it wasn't the same process in action. This was something else, and unfortunately Professor Nils had no answer to the question of what was happening.

In fact, the problem continued to be that Nils had no answer to *any* of the questions he had been presented with so far. All that the professor could tell him was common knowledge to his superiors already. Two basic facts. The creature was extremely intelligent and equally violent. The mountain of bodies this thing had created prior to its capture was evidence of this.

Nils was not a particularly brave man and was not in the habit of taking chances where it could be avoided, and merely being near to the creature filled him with barely suppressed anxiety. He peered around the Commanders shoulder to look at his specimen, his project.

He didn't like to look at it. It always looked straight back at him with fiercely malevolent eyes. Yet they didn't glow, they weren't reptilian slits or bulbous orbs, and this was perhaps the most unsettling aspect of the thing because they were merely the eyes of a human, set within the face of a man, most likely in his forties, who sported a neatly cut, probably professionally and expensively styled head of dark hair. But it wasn't human.

Far from it.

The Serasola Tower, Hanks Bay, very high up

Trey couldn't understand why Ricky insisted on using the tower as their meeting place and costume stash. Especially this high up. For a start neither of them could fly, so there was that, and between them their enhanced senses didn't allow for exceptional sight, sound, or smell beyond that of any normal person. Oh, Sure, Ricky could see in the dark but that was a big whoop when you were a thousand feet up in the air in broad daylight so they couldn't see anything more that might be happening in the city than anyone else.

It was a nice view though, if sprawling urban environments were your bag, and that's if it wasn't raining, foggy, snowing or any other of the facets of a reckless weather system plaguing the West coast these days.

Ricky was late. *As usual.*

Trey slipped a finger into the waistline of his costume and slid it around to loosen the compression of the waistband against his skin. The pants tended to rub and make him sore.

'I'm getting fat,' he thought.

He was. He had gained six pounds in the last year. Ever since his abilities had activated and scrounging around for food had become a thing of the past. His costume wasn't particularly good quality either. It wasn't as easy for a super-villain to get a wardrobe together as it was for the tighty-whiteys.

There were six businesses specializing in Hero costumes in the Bay region alone. Heroes could rock up, order bespoke gear and a week later they would be resisting fires, negating sub-zero temperatures and suppressing toxic gases, all in perfectly cut, color coordinated threads designed with the adoring consumer in mind. They even had specially designed logos.

Villains meanwhile had to pay through the nose for backstreet tailors, who had access to the kind of bio-engineered materials required and to maintain total anonymity. Sometimes you got a budding Versace, sometimes you got the guy who failed his apprenticeship through smoking crack.

Trey looked down at the logo on his chest, the one he had designed. It was a crosshair splashed with blood. He had come up with it the same time he had decided on his Villain name. He had thought it was a pretty cool super symbol. He even had a tag-line to go with it.

The Sightsmaster, he never misses. The last thing you will hear is the bullet that kills you.

It had cost him not much less than twelve hundred dollars to get the whole ensemble together. Velcro fastening sleeve compartments stitched in to carry extra rounds, a black leather harness holstered several firearms of various types, all of this part of his full outfit of black pants, black top and the obligatory hood to hide his identity.

But Ricky had said he looked like an unemployed ninja who had really let himself go. The sarcastic prick also pointed out that the red crosshair against the white circle adorning his chest was essentially a sign that stated, 'Moron. Aim here to kill.'

As if that wasn't enough Ricky also suggested that his tag line made no sense, as a bullet travelled faster than sound, so you wouldn't hear it just before it killed you, because you would already be dead.

Ricky was a top-tier asshole whose power was that he could control people for a short period. That was his thing and, grudgingly, Trey had to admit that it was an impressive ability to witness, certainly way cooler than his own mundane power.

'Proper Villain stuff,' he thought, *'like those bad Jedi, the Sith. If Obi Wan had been a Dark Jedi he would have been all 'These are the droids you're looking for.'* Waves his hand. Droids get toasted. No stupid Pod Race, no Jar Jar Binks.

'Mind you, no Empire Strikes Back either.'

Ricky never paid for a cab ride thanks to his power, and this was useful as neither of them could drive. He never paid for any shopping and if he was short of a few dollars he just asked someone in the street to give them their wallet.

There were limits though, Ricky had to be close, real close, to the person he was manipulating and the effect only lasted fifteen minutes or less. After that his marks appeared to become immune, for a while at least. Fortunately, they never remembered the incident in which they had suddenly given away their belongings.

They couldn't do banks though, or anything with *real* money. CCTV, Drumpf Drones and of course the fucking tighty-whitey's who were scampering about the city just begging to find a bad guy to pick on and show off their powers, all kept what he and Ricky could achieve as a duo down to a bare minimum. It was frustrating.

He had once thought he could make more money as a good guy, by swallowing his pride and being one of the tighties. He tried to sell his logo and ability to the corporations, ready to dance to their company tune in return for a lavish lifestyle and an action figure. But they weren't interested.

'Guys with guns are two a penny,' they said, *'they present a bad image. Men with guns conjure up images of massacres and spree killings.'* That was their explanation.

Trey knew he was being given the finger. Dismissed because, apparently, having the ability to make someone's head explode with a thought was far more palatable; one company had even called it 'chic.'

He looked out across the Hanks Bay sprawl and scanned for a target through his spare scope. There was a bird flying around the lower east side, about a half a mile away he figured. It was no more than a speck moving against the grey tower blocks, where workers wasted away their empty lives. Reaching back, he pulled the Heckler-Koch assault rifle he used for long shots into his grip. Even a veteran sniper would struggle to make his target with an assault rifle at this distance; he would need a long gun, high caliber, and a state of the art scope, but all Trey had to do was pull the trigger. It was his ability. His super power.

The bird, he couldn't tell what kind it was, moved gracefully, rising and falling with no apparent purpose other than to enjoy its incredible evolutionary gift.

'I never miss,' Trey thought.

Roughly a half a mile away from the looming bulk of the Serasola Tower a seagull, who had ridden a series of vortexes pushing warm air under its wings, careered in a lazy fashion while observing the scene below it for a suitable place to feed. Its senses sharpened for a moment as something sped by it, too fast and too small to see, the thing produced a light whistle as it passed.

A moment later a more substantial noise, that of thick glass fragmenting as a small hole was blown through it, startled the animal, and it turned violently to make sure it flew in the opposite direction of what might signify a danger. In the building behind the creature, in one of the countless plate glass windows reflecting the weak sunlight peering at the city was a hole no bigger than a dime. The glass immediately around the hole appeared frosted due to the velocity of the round impacting upon its toughened surface and from this hole erratic fracture lines reached across the pane.

Over his desk, in his office, protected from the weather and Hanks Bay smog by the punctured window, an employee of Bartlett-Pearce Conglomerate, Sponsors of the The Wild Five Heroes Response Team, stared with dead eyes at the contracts and interdepartmental memos piled upon his desk.

The shot had blown the front half of his skull out of his head and brains and blood poured down his office walls, white board and monitor.

He was the third employee who had been assassinated in as many weeks.

'I never miss.' Trey said quietly.

Professor Nils swiped through the documents on his pad. The reports he studied had come from cells across the globe, from Texas to Timbuktu and each told a similar story. He stopped at recent communiqué from Paris, France. A group, believed to be involved in a series of extremely brutal murders, all with a ritualistic element, had been discovered by a deep cover unit embedded in the city. They had enlisted the services of an Enhanced mercenary group to apprehend the cultists. These Heroes for hire went by the absurd name of Magnifiques Etalons, *Magnificent Stallions*.

Nils shook his head.

'*Assholes*,' he thought, as he read through the information.

The Stallions had descended upon an abandoned water treatment plant the cultists were using as a base of operations. Nils referred to the notes he had made in his little book, these psychopaths, the cultists, appeared to have no known affiliation to other villainous groups. This was not unusual, but it *was* odd for a criminal organisation to have no Enhanced on the payroll as muscle. A small thing, but Nils felt it had meaning somehow.

The Stallions had a member who could detect even the slightest degree of latent Enhanced ability in a fair-sized area, something Nils had been very interested in following up, unfortunately that was no longer an option.

Seeing that the cultists were merely human the Stallions launched a head-on attack. Their number included a pyromancer able to manipulate fire at will, a woman who could transform into a creature approximating a Bengal Tiger, a man called La Boa, who was so strong he could basically pick up a tank with his ass cheeks, and a smattering of other talented individuals with suitable combat powers. All told, and despite the ridiculous, name a fairly formidable group.

They were all found dead. Slaughtered to a man, and tiger. Somehow the cultists had dispatched an entire team of Enhanced without firing a shot or even possessing their own powers. Further to this there was evidence of the Stallions having been subject to either torture, or possibly some form of ritualistic dismembering.

Nils swiped the Paris report away and considered the next. Champagne, Urbana, Illinois. An Amish youth had been reported missing. When he was finally located, he was in no less than thirty parts. His family had kept the young man's burgeoning power a secret, unable to decide if his mutation was a gift from God or a curse from the Devil. It was like the Frenchman, he looked at his notes again, *La Boa,* the boy had incredible strength, and apparently had been holding sections of a barns up by himself as others worked upon them.

'*Probably quite glamorous for the Amish,*' Nils thought.

In each of the reports the common theme was the ritualistic murder of Enhanced individuals and no obvious signs of how they were subdued. There was also one other thing that tied them together, a name.

Nils made a gesture on the pad with his fingers and a video link to the holding chamber opened on the screen. The creature was still sat at the table, as it had been earlier. It rarely moved from it. It rarely moved at all in fact, and it certainly *never* spoke.

He returned his attention to the pad. While these varied groups of cultists appeared to have no name or title of their own they were known throughout the underworld as *Ghouls,* and while it was only high profile victims who made it to the desks of the company's investigators these people were well known for murder generally. They didn't steal; they didn't defraud, blackmail or threaten. They just killed people. Frequently.

They were tough to find as well. Bordering on impossible to detect, absolutely impossible to follow. This is why *she* had been brought in to help. *The Witch.*

How Carver had managed to persuade her to assist him was still a mystery to Nils. The girl was smart, frighteningly so, able, and most enigmatic of all, she was not Enhanced. Or at least this is what she claimed. He had no reason not to believe her despite wanting too.

The Witch had showed them the symbols and how to prepare them. She had provided various concoctions, *potions* Nils supposed, to be used in subduing the creature. The holding unit it was currently residing in was covered wall to wall in mysterious runes. Archaic patterns which Nils thought occasionally altered their form. They unnerved him. She unnerved him. Nils thought no one on Earth had more reason to be concerned about the Witch than he did. The Enhanced didn't worry him, at least not biologically.

The Enhanced he could understand, to a certain extent they were just the products of nature and therefore measurable by science, true it was science of such a high level that the words of Arthur C Clarke often came to mind, 'any sufficiently advanced technology is indistinguishable from magic,' but still, it was just science.

The creature in the cell however was alien to all of his learning and all of the laws of his universe as he understood them, at least so far. There were similarities he thought, for a start it needed to feed, but it didn't feed on flesh, or drink water, or even require sunlight. How it was feeding was a mystery, but patterns had been witnessed suggesting the thing at least took in some form of sustenance.

For example, it would spend a week or so looking robust and healthy then it would begin to grow listless and look markedly weak, then... poof... it was fine, and back to its usual, malignantly grinning self. Yes, it definitely fed in some way.

Then there was the problem of killing it. Radiation didn't affect it, nor did any of the elements. During the first attempts to capture the creature it had been shot, stabbed, torched and there had even been an attempt to crush it, and all to no avail other than perhaps causing it some inconvenience.

The Witch had been prepared to help them destroy it, until she had discovered the companies plan had been to capture it for study all along.

Nils shuddered. That hadn't gone down well at all. Words had been exchanged. Things had gotten unpleasant. She could be a handful.

The creature did obey some laws though. This was what was possibly the strangest. For a start, it made no attempt to remove the runes about its cell. It was as though something prevented it from doing so. The various glyphs were produced from nothing more than stencils designed by the Witch, and yet this ungodly thing could do nothing but sit at its table and stare through the one-way mirrored window, which clearly wasn't one way to *it*.

Nils leaned back in his chair and as he did so the creature looked up at one of the camera domes. It stared directly at him. There were eight individual domes in that room yet it knew exactly which one to look at every time it wanted to give Nils the shivers.

'Stare all you want fucker.' Nils said.

It did.

Hanks Bay, near Bob's Pizza, you know, the place where The Dark Dervish got wasted by the Goon Gang.

Ricky hadn't stopped talking since their meeting at the Tower. Whenever they met it was always the same, how awesome he was, how many girls he had banged since he last charged his phone, how much cash he taken off some guy in the street, how popular he was with pretty much everyone.

Trey really couldn't see what the attraction could be, Ricky was the most vacuous and boring fucking individual he had ever met. He was good looking he supposed, he had that chin, the one that all the jocks had, a straight nose, clear skin, dark eyes with matching eyebrows. Even his stubble was pretty cool, uniform and dark like a sexy shadow across his jaw. But underneath the poster-boy looks was a massive, uninteresting pile of slug shit.

'Really, two chicks? Nice going Ricky.' Trey said with absolutely no sincerity, having just caught the end of Ricky's current anecdote concerning his morning.

'DON'T CALL ME BY MY NAME ASSHOLE!' Ricky bawled. He gripped Treys arm bringing him to a halt.

'Sorry Ri... man, I forgot.'

'What's my fucking name?' Ricky demanded, he stepped in close and Trey knew that this was a warning that if he didn't play ball any second now he could be running up the street naked and laughing like a loon.

'Dream Machine man, you're Dream Machine... I just forgot is all.'

'Why?' Trey asked.

'Wha?'

'Why am I Dream Machine?'

Ricky's grip tightened, he wasn't super strong but he was two hours a day in the gym strong, he was Pilates and spinning class fit, so it still hurt.

'Cos you're dreamy looking man, and a machine in the sack, a regular Terminator.' Trey said, with as much conviction as he could muster.

'Yeah.' Ricky said, nodding, he loosened his grip a little.

'A fucking Terminator.' He smiled and the hand gripping Trey's arm loosened and then slapped him on the back. As though the sudden episode had never happened Ricky resumed his jocular demeanour.

'Come on dude, we need to head over to Rupes, I got us a deal.' Ricky said.

'A deal?'

'Yeah. I got an interested party. They wanna make use of the Dream Machine and his trusty sidekick The Sightmaster!'

Trey bristled, 'Hey, come on, I'm not a sidekick dude.'

Ricky broadened his smile, 'Man, course not, I'm just fucking with you.'

He gave Trey a playful punch on his shoulder. 'Come on, let's go rap with this guy, see what we can score.'

Trey nodded and they continued on their way. He wished he had his guns with him, but they were way up on the Serasola Tower, hidden away with his costume. It hadn't slipped his notice that Ricky was only this high level of asshole with him when he was out of character.

'Not so fucking tough when I'm strapped' Trey thought, *'Only talking shit about me when I'm close enough to be mind-fucked.'*

It was getting to be too much. The insults, the jibes, the constant belittling of him were wearing thin. Ricky had always been there for him in the past he had thought, that they had both developed super powers had been really cool. But something else had developed in Trey which he was glad he hadn't shared with Ricky, not a power but just as valuable, his observational skill and ability to step back and consider his place in the world had grown.

Trey accepted that he wasn't square jawed or particularly tall, that his skin was a little dry near his nose and his facial hair was restricted to an inconsequential tuft beneath his average chin.

'But I'm pretty smart and I'm quick on my toes in a tight situation, and I have a fucking SUPER POWER for Christ's sake.'

Trey fought hard against his incomprehensible dependence on the acceptance of a friend who had only ever used him every single day. But the world was a scary place and without Ricky the chances were that it might be even scarier, and so Trey dropped his head a little and walked on quietly as Ricky talked, and talked, and talked.

Offices of Bartlett-Pearce Conglomerate, Sponsors of the The Wild Five Heroes Response Team. The same building in which Trey murdered someone earlier in the story, much higher up though.

'Another one Rod. Right here. Right here in the fucking building. This is *not* what I call progress.'

Eddie Banes, Bartlett-Pearce's Director of Marketing jabbed a finger firmly onto a slim stack of papers on his desk. The topmost page bore a photograph held in place with a single paperclip. The image was one of a couple of thousand like it, an employee, executive class, he could this tell by the nimbus blue background the person would was photographed against.

Rod Raynes was tempted to lean forward and slip the little photo from the grip of the paperclip. He wanted to take a good look at who he had failed to protect this time.

'I know, I'm sorry Eddie I really am, we all are.' Rod said, as his eyes flicked about the room looking anywhere other than at the tight-lipped face of the Director.

'Sorry?' Banes nodded and pursed his lips. 'I'll bet you are sorry. However, my worry is that you aren't *twenty eight million dollars* sorry Rod. My *concern* is that the twenty-eight million you and your colleagues received last year in Bartlett-Pearce sponsorship isn't money well spent.'

'Eddie, we...' Rod started, but was cut off as Banes stood.

'No more excuses Rod, no more.' Banes chopped his hand to the side. 'I want this prick apprehended, better yet I want him dead! I've had to triple my personal security. Jesus, it's getting that I can't take a shit without having four guys stood around my fucking cubicle.'

'With respect sir we can't just kill someone we...'

'Rod, twenty-eight million dollars says you can. Twenty-eight million says that if I ask you and your squad of ultimate assholes to run down Central Avenue naked, with firecrackers up your asses, you'll fucking do it. No questions asked. Got that?'

Rod stiffened. Banes was prone to quick tempers and harsh words but he was moving into the red zone. He would take any amount of punishment to be dished out but he wasn't prepared to have the team dragged into the pit with him. He stepped forward to offer some show of defiance.

'Sir, the team have worked hard to apprehend this sniper. We have explored every avenue open to us but the facts are that he is operating at a distance, we have no word of affiliation with any organization and his ammunition is incredibly common so we can't narrow our search. If it were military grade, or exotic in some way I'm sure we could get to him faster.'

It was all true. The team had pinned their hopes on the rounds being used by the killer as a road map to him, or at least to point the way. This had not been the case. However, it had indicated one thing for certain, some kind of Enhanced ability was being employed. The shots had been fired at a distance that would have required an exceptionally well trained marksman but further to that there was no possible way the kind of low end rounds being used would have caused the damage they did. It was as though there had been no drop in velocity at all, which over a distance of half a mile was beyond all physical law. Which meant Enhanced powers.

Banes sat, but appeared no less agitated. 'Find him,' he said.

'We will sir.'

'Kill him.' Banes ordered, and his eyes underlined that this was non-negotiable, not a request or something to be considered as a possible outcome. It was to be a done thing. A fact.

Rod said nothing but gave a slight nod of his head. He turned and left the office, knowing full well he had left his balls and dignity in there with the Director of Operations.

The moment he left the Bartlett-Pearce building he called Phantom Lady, also known as Vanessa Peel.

'Hey Rod, what's up?' Vanessa said.

Rod held his breath for a moment, he did this almost every time he heard Vanessa speak for the first time in a while. He had been in love with her since the first moment they had met, but Rod knew it was a hopeless infatuation. Vanessa was half his age, she was beautiful, and in every sense of the word. She was funny, kind, exciting and sensitive. He was a tired, cynical man of fifty-two and all he had to offer anyone was the ability to punch his way through a steel wall. Why the hell would a dream girl waste time on a loser like him?

'Hey, Vanessa, listen you need to gather the team. Banes is on the warpath.'

'Jesus, I take it this is to do with the sniper?'

'Yeah.'

There was a short silence and Rod imagined Vanessa lying on her bed with her phone to her ear. His brain conjured up a silky teddy rippling across her body as she moved.

'OK Pops, I'll get the guys. Where are meeting?'

'Better make it the Five Building, Banes will want the press to see us assembling. I'll call Channel Zero.'

'Sure, I'll get my ass in gear, get my war-paint on. See you later.'

'See you.' Rod said.

'*Pops.*' His ego made sure he felt the weight of the implication. She meant well. He was the oldest, the leader, their Captain. Yeah, she meant well, but it depressed him so much that he could already feel the need to get a drink.

'What a day,' he said, as he put his phone away. 'What a fucking day.

The West Side Olympic Stadium, Hanks Bay

Trey was completely unsurprised that the stadium, which had been, for two glorious weeks, the jewel in the crown of the city during his nations hosting of the Olympic games, was now a base of operations for villains. After all, the entire thing had been built on corruption in the first place.

There had been a great deal of talk of what would happen after the games. Great plans had been floated of retail developments, living space, nature parks and community enterprise. Of course, that had all been bullshit. The second the last race had been run and the events had moved on to the Lincoln Stadium, another Mafia funded arena, the doors were boarded up and the building left to rot.

With the coming of the Enhancing its use even as a sporting venue was gone. No one wanted to watch normal people run, or throw, or fight anymore. This stadium, once considered vast was now far too small to accommodate both the powers of the competitors and the crowds that flocked to see them.

Many Enhanced could throw a javelin half a mile, they could get around a thousand-meter track so fast that a whole day's worth of events would be over in an hour, so the organizers had spiced it up a bit.

Now the stadiums were huge obstacle courses complete with potentially lethal traps. Cameras covered every square inch, and the perils of the athletes were transmitted in glorious 3D via Pay per View to an insatiable audience.

These Super-Stadia were brought about by senators, who in turn had been bought off by the bribes and threats of criminal organizations and equally corrupt corporations. They granted the leviathan constructions, which swallowed entire communities and then left the buildings to die.

Trey and Ricky stood in the car park. Itself a vision of post-apocalyptic abandonment. Each wore a balaclava. A token gesture towards hiding their identity. It cut at Trey that his token gesture was also a part of his costume. He really wanted something tailor made. Something with a built-in communications unit and sensors.

It was quiet. The noise of the city was dampened by rain falling over it and the storm threatened to move towards the stadium.

'I'm gonna get fucking wet.' Trey thought. He wanted this to be over quickly.

The panel of a boarded-up entrance moved to the side and two figures emerged. Ricky saw them first, he touched Treys arm.

The figures walked slowly towards them.

'Fuckers are wearing dresses.' Ricky sneered, 'Are they faggots?'

Trey mentally shook his head. Ricky was a bigoted fuck, and why not, he was clearly trying to possess every awful attribute a human being could muster. He squinted and saw the two were wearing something like robes. He rifled through his memories, *cowls,* they were more like cowls.

As they neared one of the figures raised a hand.

'Greetings, Dream Machine and Sightmaster,' he said.

'Creepy,' Trey thought. The two men looked thin, underfed.

'Hey,' Ricky said.

The men stopped.

Trey stared, puzzled as they did something with their hands, each of them, they made some odd gestures in unison, then continued towards him and Ricky. They stopped within an arm's length, personal space clearly not high on their agenda.

'Our name is Legion,' the one who had issued the greeting said, and indicated the two of them.

'You're both named Legion?' Ricky asked.

'Yes,' said the other robed man, 'for we are many.'

'Right.' Ricky replied.

Trey was happy to let his friend do the talking, not that Ricky would allow it to be any other way.

'We are pleased that you have agreed to come to us. We believe we can offer you great fortune and power.'

This was the one to the left speaking so Trey decided he would be called Lefty, he thought they could be clones, or at least related, but he quickly realized that it was just the gaunt look and lack of hair that gave them a similar appearance.

'Well that's what we're here for buddy,' Ricky replied with his usual cocky self-assurance.

And then something strange occurred.

Ricky went quiet and his breathing became shallow. Trey immediately knew what he was doing, he was attempting to control one of the Legion people, most likely the one he decided to call Lefty, who was directly in front of Ricky. He had witnessed his partner in crime do this a hundred times or more and the effect was always the same. The target would look confused, their jaw might slacken, and they would blink as though their eyelids were heavy. Then they would do whatever Ricky desired of them.

What was strange however, was that nothing happened at all. Whatever it was that went through Ricky's mind when he had control of someone must have flagged back to him that it hadn't worked. Trey watched carefully as Ricky frowned, took a step back and grew quiet.

'We would ask you to come of your own free will to the Stadium this evening. There we will discuss what plans we have and how you gentlemen can become a part of our organization.' Lefty said in his quiet monotone voice.

Ricky remained silent. Trey thought he had better step in to keep control of the conversation.

'Why tonight? We're here right now.'

The other Legion man chirped in. 'We needed to be sure that you were prepared to come of course, and at this time we are not fully prepared for a meeting. You must understand that when dealing with powerful individuals like you and your colleague we must be satisfied that our safety is ensured.'

'We're not here to fuck with you man.' Trey replied, but given that fuck-head Ricky had just tried to mind control one of them they probably had a point.

'Of course, but when you operate at our level you will understand that one can never be too cautious.' Lefty gave Ricky a look that dared him to question that statement.

'Fair enough.' Trey said, 'We'll come back tonight.'

'At 10pm if you will.' Lefty said.

'10pm. We'll be here,' Trey replied, 'and we would appreciate it if we could actually discuss some business, rather than having a 'getting to know' you chat in a car park.'

The Legion men nodded as one.

Trey felt Ricky tug on his arm. He turned to face him.

'Let's go.' Ricky said.

Even with Ricky's face obscured by his balaclava Trey could see that he was worried. He turned back to Lefty and his buddy.

'We'll be here tonight, 10pm, don't leave us out here jerking off.' Trey said sharply.

Another nod. The Legion men turned and walked slowly back to the stadium.

'Let's get the fuck out of here.' Ricky grunted, already walking away as he said it.

Trey jogged to catch up.

'What's the problem?' he asked, already knowing the answer.

'Those fuckers. I couldn't control them. Either of them.' Ricky sounded like a child who had been scolded for not doing his chores. 'I couldn't get into their heads; it was like they had a wall built around them.' He pulled off his balaclava and Trey did likewise.

'Wow,' Trey said.

It was genuinely surprising. He had never seen a person block Ricky before and it had clearly affected him, but he couldn't resist chiding the mighty Dream Machine,

'That must really burst your bubble Rick.'

Ricky rounded on Trey at this. He gripped Treys collar in a fist and brought his face in close.

'What the fuck do you mean you little prick. D'you think it's funny? D'you think you can fucking laugh at me?'

Trey said nothing. Ricky's eyes were wild and tears were threatening to spill from them.

'I dare you to laugh at me you pathetic piece of shit, try it, go on. You'll wake up with a crowd around you, wondering why you just fucked a dog in the street.'

Trey remained silent. Ricky was bigger than him, stronger than him and really could just snatch his control over himself away. Better to let his anger dissipate than risk riling him up by trying to calm him down.

'I thought not,' Ricky snarled. He released Trey's collar and shoved him away.

Something caught Ricky's eye. Trey followed his gaze and saw a dog, a scrawny brown thing scavenging amongst the piles of junk that had been tipped around the place.

Ricky picked up a fist sized piece of rubble. The mutt was sniffing at something, its drooped tail wagged a little. Perhaps it had found some carrion or an abandoned snack. Ricky drew back his arm to throw the rock at the dog.

Trey thought that at this range there was a good chance Ricky would hit, and a rock that size would hurt or possibly injure the animal. There was really no need for Ricky to take his frustration out on it. It was yet more behavior typical of his sadistic, bullying nature.

Ricky wore a gritted smile as he reached far back and then hurled the rock at the dog. His aim was true, the animal was close, side on, and he had the strength to give the shot sufficient force to make sure a few of the dog's ribs would crack when it impacted onto its side.

But Trey caught the missile as it left Ricky's fingers. He took the rock in his mind, felt its shape and weight and moved with it. To him it wasn't fast, it wasn't hurtling through the air. It was as though time had slowed down, or perhaps his mind was moving at an insane speed and so leaving everything else standing.

28

About half way to the target Trey began to add a little curve to the rock's trajectory. There was a tin can behind the dog and this became the missiles new destination. Trey guided it into the can. It struck, making a startling 'THUNK' noise. The can rattled across the ground and the dog bolted.

Trey blinked as he heard Ricky shout.

'FUCK!'

'What just happened,' Trey thought. *'What the fuck?'*

Ricky stomped off, back towards the city. Trey looked at the stone lying close to where the dog had been. He focused and stared hard at it. He screwed up his face and tried to cast his thoughts around it.

Nothing happened. It was just a rock. But something *had* happened. He had felt it. A sensation of *flight*, of what it must be like to hurtle through the air. A few Enhanced could do it to varying degrees. Captain Courage, leader of the The Wild Five was always seen in the papers zipping from building to building. Trey had seen him close up once, he had landed outside the children's home on Lindsay Street. He was carrying a huge cardboard cheque for 50,000 dollars, donated by Bartlett & Pearce. There was a rumor that the cheque was being given as one of the home's kids had been killed during some incident in which the TW5 were involved. But rumors about Corporations and Superhero Teams were like assholes, they were everywhere. Trey only wished he had been in costume that day. He would have put a bullet right through that cardboard bribery certificate and into Captain Courage's prostituted heart.

Trey turned from the rock and looked towards the retreating figure of Ricky. He would keep his distance for a while. Ricky was mad as hell and when he was like this people suffered and sometimes it was him. A brief vision of Ricky's head exploding like a watermelon flashed through his mind.

Trey shrugged and slowly followed his partner into the city.

The TW5 Building, Downtown Hanks Bay – You can follow the adventures of the West Coast's Number One Super Hero Team via B&P's low cost Pay Per View Subscription offer. Terms and Conditions apply.

Rod landed on the roof of the TW5 building unseen, even by the Drumpf Drones and SpyCams. He had absolutely no doubt that Banes would have wanted him to enter through the main doors on the ground, but the press was out in force and even the Paparazzi, camped out on the perimeter, were unusually agitated.

This hadn't been the case this morning when he had dropped by the office to collect his new costume. They had all been issued the latest version of the team uniform, featuring its new, more vibrant colors and a bold stripe that slashed across the chest.

'We wanted something *wild* and *exciting*.' A marketing exec whose face was bloated with the amount of Botox injected into it had said. Rod thought he looked like a talking potato. He knew marketing had precisely no interest in whether the kit was wild and exciting. They just wanted something slightly different to the last costume. They wanted something that all the little kids and wannabe Enhanced would crave and covet despite having shelled out hard earned dollars for cheap imported material stitched together by eight-year-old kids, just three months earlier.

'Captain, our data shows that we have a growing demographic amongst the male Latino population aged 16-35 since the inclusion of Fire Swan in the line-up.' Her super power was that she could make fire engulf her hands. That was it. Seemingly at will Swan could have flames flickering from her fingers and palms. Rod had to admit that it looked pretty cool, especially with her body and her looks as the backdrop, but that was the sum of her talent. Her hands caught fire.

She couldn't throw the flames or make them extend into a lance of burning fury, and she also had trouble putting them out. They didn't just 'flame off,' she had to wait until they died down.

She was a nice kid though. Rod liked her. She always called him Captain, or Sir, which was respectful, but she was practically useless in any other sense, to the team at least.

The guy she had replaced, Marvin Boyd, AKA King Beast, had been a real asset. A tough motherfucker imported from Harlem. He had an affinity with animals, could communicate with them on some fucked up level that no one could even guess at, he had a sidekick too, a Kodiak Bear that was pretty much his best friend.

B&P used the animal as part of Beast's marketing profile but they never let it out with him on a mission. No way they were going to underwrite a wild animal running through the city regardless of its connection to Marvin. Instead it was kept at the Hanks Bay Zoo as a star attraction. Marvin had complained at first but the money spoke louder than any empathy he had with the animal.

Marvin had died in a road traffic accident three months ago. B&P had tried to sex it up. That King Beast had been targeted by a mysterious and shadowy organisation related to an unnamed crime syndicate. Pretty vague even by their standards but they had invested a lot of money in King Beast toys, thirst and were even looking into animated series with a card game associated with it. They wanted a return. The truth was that Marvin had been texting his dealer while already coked up at the wheel of his Lexus. He had crossed the central reservation and ploughed into an oncoming semi. He had to be scraped from the interior.

Rod visited the bear every week that he could after that especially as B&P ceased funding its deluxe habitat once King Beast was written off. He had no empathy talent or ability to converse on any level with animals, it was difficult enough to engage with humans these days, but he did think that it recognised him. It looked sad and it looked lonely. He thought it might also be angry and so perhaps he did share some empathy with it. He slipped the keeper a hundred bucks each time, to 'upgrade' it's diet and to ensure it was given a little extra attention. He hoped someone out there might do the same for him some day.

Banes had brought in two potential new members, one of whom would eventually replace Marvin. Fire Swan was pushed forward for her obvious sex appeal, leaving the other in the wings. A person who Rod thought would make a far better addition to the squad. A truly Enhanced named Alex Peacock.

Alex could run at near Cheetah speed. He had been clocked at fifty miles per hour over flat ground, but that was only where his talent began. Alex Peacock, now called Velocity, phased between dimensions. Upon reaching the top end of his physical speed he somehow gained the ability to slip into what the Bartlett and Pearce R&D boffins were calling 'Null Space.'

To the naked eye it appeared that Alex, who was already exceeding the speed of any non-Enhanced human, was moving faster than the speed of sound. In actual fact, he was covering large distances in Null-space and then reappearing in our dimension so fast that the illusion of supersonic speed was created. Rod could barely even comprehend what that meant in terms of the science involved but for the team he was a truly rapid response unit ready to help protect humanity.

But Alex was Black and the Black demographic wasn't an 'optimal' market at this time. Alex was also forty-two years old and very few consumers were buying into Heroes in that age bracket and to cap it off Alex was gay, so he might as well have had a super power that burned orphans alive because Bartlett & Pearce represented the most right wing sector of American enterprise on the west coast. Even the Ku Klux Klan had more liberal values. Bartlett and Pearce decided that the under-age porn star look would serve them far more profits than a middle-aged homosexual with a desire to save lives.

Rod kept in touch with him. Alex was always ready to help in any way he could and he found him very easy to talk to. For the latter he was most grateful, especially when all he could see as he raged in the 'release room' B&P had built to allow him to exercise his super-strength, was a perpetually running river of Jack Daniels.

When he entered the meeting room Rod saw that the team had already arrived. Here they all were again, five high functioning Enhanced, all under contract to a multi-billion-dollar corporation that was only interested in how much cash they could make from its youngest member's breasts. It sickened him.

Fire Swan was sat at the large hexagon table, looking like all of those billions of dollars, at least if highly sexualised teens were your thing. She was attentive to all that was going on in the TW5 meeting room, she was sweet, polite and almost certainly a virgin. Rod wondered how B&P were going to market that. He had no doubt that they would get around to it before it was too late.

Phantom Lady was stood behind a chair directly opposite Swan. She was in conversation with the inimitable Dragons Claw, Chu Wan. Chu was a serious individual. He took his role as a defender of humanity as far more than a PR role. Considerate, polite, sensitive and an off the chart kick ass martial artist.

Rod couldn't fathom why Chu chose to accept the five-year contract Bartlett & Pearce had given him. Marvin had his drugs, Swan would have a modelling and acting career as soon as she finished her term, Phantom Lady was bored, she did a few drugs but wasn't yet the addict level Marvin had reached, and then there was Hyper-Ton. Hyper, or Frank Mitchell as his driver's license read, just liked to smash things. To him the contract was five years of being able to beat the fuck out of people with minimum legal comeback. There was no love lost between him and Rod and they kept their distance.

In fact, within the team, Rod only really communicated with Vanessa, despite it adding to his depression.

'Hello everyone thanks for coming at such short notice,' Rod said, 'I saw Director Banes earlier today and...' he stopped. Something was wrong with the expressions on his colleague's faces.

'What's the matter?' he asked

Phantom Lady stepped forwards.

'You haven't been told?' she said

'Told what?' Rod asked, puzzled.

'Banes called here twenty minutes ago, says they have the identity of the shooter.'

'Really, because I just...?'

'Uh huh, name, date of birth, address, everything. Seems some anonymous civilian dropped the dime on him. It's a kid named Trey Storno.'

'You've got to be fucking kidding me,' Rod replied, astonished.

Chu stepped forward, 'Captain, we have been informed that this person works alongside another Enhanced, one Richard Mayweather, who has been suspected of multiple rapes and other acts of sexual assault. Neither is registered. They call themselves Sightmaster and Dream Machine.'

Rod almost laughed, 'Dream Machine? Are you guys fucking with me?'

Swan stood, 'No sir, Director Banes has sent us surveillance tapes and background documents that have been tied in with the activities of these two.'

'In twenty minutes?' Rod asked, still not believing that the man he had been trying to locate for six months and had finally caught a scent of was now a cab ride away.

Phantom Lady continued the series of seismic shocks

'Yes, apparently, a complete file was delivered to his personal email. Someone has obviously been monitoring the suspects.'

'Well I'll be Goddamned,' Rod said.

'Who gives a fuck where the info came from?' Hyper-Ton said, 'Let's go and smash these fucks into the floor and collect that bonus.'

Biohazard Quarantine and Containment facility, Arizona, Professor Nils study. What a guy.

An audible alert chimed through the speakers. Nils looked up from his reports and at the larger TV screen in his study. A news report.

He was subscribed to over a hundred and fifty Pay Per View channels that featured Enhanced in some form or another. There were a startlingly large number of porn oriented stations but these rarely occupied him. He had no real interest in how long an Enhanced man could keep an erection and certainly no wish to witness a performing vagina.

Those on show were essentially at the absolute rock bottom of Enhanced life, riddled with narcotics and disease and not even useful as test subjects. Every now and then some unusual ability or talent might be observed and Nils would make notes, but this was rarely worth the effort.

There were various other entertainment channels. He had access to a few underground streams that featured illicit fights, often between Enhanced and occasionally with animals thrown in for good measure. All very base stuff, evidence that despite the evolutionary leap it had enjoyed mankind was basically still dragging its knuckles along to the next fuck fest.

Nils picked up one of the remotes on his desk and pressed a button. The screen flicked to one of the sponsored Super Team channels that had an 'ALERT' signal showing. It was The Wild Five Station and according to the sliding graphics at the bottom of the video stream the team were about to make an arrest. It was all live of course, well, bar the ten second delay required by law in case of something happening which people shouldn't be seeing.

Although Nils wasn't entirely sure what that could be these days. Perhaps a politician telling the truth.

'Hmm… West Coast?' Nils asked himself.

He turned the sound up as the picture of a crowd gathered around a large modern structure with a high-tech billboard showing the members of the team in various action poses, switched to a studio set with a tick all the boxes looking anchorman about to begin talking.

'We have just been informed that West Coast Super Team, The Wild Five, are about to go into action against a deadly duo who have been terrorizing the good citizens of Hanks Bay for the last six months.'

Nils nodded. *'Yes, yes, West Coast.'* He liked to be right.

'The individuals are believed to be Richard Mayweather and Trey Storno. Both in possession of Enhanced talents used for murderous ends.'

'Fucking marketing imbeciles.' Nils muttered. He knew it would be the work of the sponsors letting that information out. Let the bad guys know the cavalry is coming so they have time to get ready, then it will be a better fight, better television.

'According to our sources the full Five will be making the arrest, such is the danger presented by these diabolical super-villains.'

Nils shook his head. 'Super villains, why are they super?' he said to the screen. 'I've never fucking heard of them you dick head.' He shook his head, 'Unbelievable.'

Two photographs flashed up on the screen. Both looked like college yearbook shots. On the left a scraggly looking youth with bad skin and bored eyes, under the image a title, The Sightmaster. On the right a moderately handsome young man with a chin that was slightly too big to make the look work, and a punch me in the face expression. Under his image was the name, Dream Machine.

Nils laughed. 'Ha! What a cunt.' He slapped his hand down on his desk. He decided he wanted to see this show and leaned back into his chair.

Sponsored super teams were followed everywhere by drones, helicopters and swarms of paparazzi. They were the new rock stars. Men with chiselled abs enhanced by carefully sculpted bio-engineered materials. Women who were painted up to look like every man's wet dream and with bodies that fitted the exact proportions that the media insisted were those of a goddess.

As publicity shots of the team appeared on screen Nils had to admit that Fire Swan and Phantom Lady did look pretty fucking hot. He tapped onto the tablet he had been working on and brought up registration information on the two women. Phantom Lady was interesting and Nils was sure he had reviewed her file before. She could pass through solid objects, had a strong resistance to elemental and kinetic damage plus enhanced vision and aural capacity. Certainly a Class A specimen. He made a note to look into her situation a little more closely once he could free up some time.

He studied the other, Fire Swan. Seventeen years old. Could make her hands spontaneously emit flames. Limited in both range and ability to control the output. No other known Enhanced traits.

'Well, at least you are very pretty my dear,' Nils said, as he closed her file.

He knew the others well enough as he had followed their exploits before Bartlett and Pearce had contracted them. Dragons Claw had the usual strength, speed and kinetic resistance of the average Enhanced, but his martial arts knowledge pushed him into a higher category of superhuman. Nils knew a few Enhanced that had pretty much super-duper everything but couldn't fight their way out a wet paper bag.

Hyper-ton was amongst those ranks. Incredibly strong and with the ability to take tremendous amounts of punishment, but the man had no finesse, certainly no actual intelligence with which to channel the products of his evolutionary lottery win. Nils had tested his IQ during registration and judged that if the man had been green skinned he could have passed as a vegetable.

Finally, there was their leader. Captain Courage, a further ludicrous example of corporate marketing to the lowest common denominator and another individual with incredible gifts that were squandered on an alcoholic, manic depressive. Nils had forgotten the man's name and so scrolled up to his general details.

Rodney Raynes.

Former Occupation – Military (see assoc files)
Status – Widower

Latent Enhanced ability/talents

Strength – 5 on the Dawkins Scale
Vision – Extended, Approx. 3 on the Dawkins Scale
Meta Regeneration – Approx. 3 on the Dawkins Scale
Flight : Limited (see evaluation)

Deemed unsuitable for further study due to deep unresolved psychological issues and alcoholism. Mentally unstable, however removed from danger watch list as subject is now under the jurisdiction of Bartlett & Pearce Conglomerate and their Enhanced Monitoring program.

At the side of the typewritten report Nils recognised his own handwriting, it read *'their problem now.'*

'And here they come!' the anchorman's eyes slipped to the right, observing his own little TV screen. Behind him a visual appeared in a rectangular box, a drone-cam view of the TW5 building from about thirty feet in the air. A long black line appeared across the building, the hangar door was opening. The huge door slid smoothly down to reveal the tip of the TW5 Fast Response Jet. This carried the team to their missions at supersonic speeds, was capable of vertical take-off and landing and looked very, very cool.

'the familiar sight of the TW5 Fast Response Jet, TW6 to you and I folks, is about to leave the hanger and do we see... YES, there he is, Captain Courage flies out before the vehicle. Captain Courage, or TW1, is known for his strength, hyper enhanced vision, ability to fly and of course tremendous patriotism and leadership.'

Nils snorted. Raynes could fly for about three to five minutes then he was done, grounded for at least an hour. He knew the second that jet was out of general view of the public the Captain would be clambering inside it before he fell to his death.

Nils couldn't deny that being able to fly unaided, even for a short period was impressive, but he was no Jetstream or Nimbus, the duo in Britain who could actually move through the ionosphere, *'now that's flying'* he thought. The Brits had some very interesting subjects and he wished he could get his hands on them.

'There they go folks. I'm being told that all of the TW5 are en route to their mission and that we will have full video coverage of it. For all subscription rates just press the red button. If you are already a subscriber to our premium service, you may want to upgrade to our Platinum 3D and HD Dolby platform as this promises to be a real show.'

Nils shook his head and tutted. *'A real show, one of them has hands that catch fire, whoopy fucking doo.'*

He knew how this was going to pan out. Dragons Claw and Hyper-ton would beat the living shit out of the alleged bad guys and Phantom Lady and Fire Swan would prance around looking sexy. If they stage managed it right they would all get their costumes torn a little to offer a bit of titillation. Captain Courage would drag the unconscious villains towards the Jet and look directly at one of their drone-cams and say, *'sleep easy folks, two more villainous scum brought to justice by The Wild Five. We don't sleep so that you and your blessed families can. Don't forget to subscribe by pushing the red button.'*

'Or some other such shit.' Nils said out loud.

There was a knock at his door, which startled him a little.

'Who is it? I'm busy.'

'Carver,' came the reply.

Nils sighed and sat upright.

'Come in.'

Carver entered, he looked serious, but then he always looked serious. He pointed at the monitor displaying the TW5 Jet moving into position.

'This is the West Coast team isn't it? Hanks Bay?'

'Yah, The Wild Five. Nothing exciting.'

'Bring up Cell 12.' Carver said.

Nils's mouth went dry. Cell 12 was *his* Cell. He tapped his pad and one of the Camera Domes in its Cell showed the creature at his table. Its head was bowed and its hands spread either side of the table, palms face down.

'It's done that before. It's like its thinking or praying.' Nils said.

'Yes.' Carver said, 'but there is something else, the Commander reached over Nils shoulder and tapped onto Nil's pad. The professor flinched a little. He didn't like his stuff touched, although technically it wasn't really *his* stuff, but still.

'You remember when some kind of altercation took place in New Hampshire? A bunch of Enhanced all went at it in an abandoned theme park. Total bloodbath. Every one of them died at the scene.'

'Of course.' Nils replied.

'Take a look at this.' Carver jabbed a finger down on the pad. The frozen image on the screen began to play. It was the creature, still in his cell, still in his suit with his hundred-dollar haircut and manicured nails. His head was bowed, his hands spread to either side of the table.

Nils looked at the time stamp running at the bottom right of the video.

'Same date as the Hampshire Incident.' Nils said

'Same time.' Carver replied.

———

'Really?' Nils said carefully. That is... interesting.'

Carver tapped at the pad again and a new image, strikingly similar to the previous one came up.

'January 28th, twenty two hundred hours,'

Nils raised his eyebrows. He knew that date well. 'Rome?'

'Rome,' Carver echoed. He pressed play. The creature was in the same position. 'The same time that eight quite exceptional Enhanced slaughtered each other inside the Coliseum.'

'Good god.' Nils said.

'*You* spotted this?' Nils asked, Carver nodded.

'This thing doesn't do much other than stare at you like you are its next meal...' Carver pointed at the thing on the screen, '...and this.'

There was no chance he was going to admit this to Carver but Nils had completely breezed past this behaviour, assuming the thing must be sleeping or recovering its energy in some way, like humans. But it wasn't human. That Carver was the one who had seen some kind of connection with outside events made him feel somewhat of a cunt. He had to try and save face.

'I have been performing investigations in this behaviour Commander but it appears you are a step ahead me,' Nils offered a small smile, '*more like a fucking country mile.*'

'That doesn't matter,' Carver said brusquely, 'what is important here Nils is that we study this. If there is a link here, some connection we have overlooked we need to get all the data we can.'

'Of course.' Nils replied. He knew that Carver didn't believe him. '*Shit*' he thought.

Carver walked across Nil's study and dragged a chair next to the Professor.

'Ah, looks like we have a movie date Commander.' Nils said.

Carver gave him a look that had sent better men to a firing squad.

The West Coast Olympic Stadium, 10pm.

Trey and Ricky approached the Stadium cautiously. There were no exterior lights on, nothing to guide them other than the turnstile entrance with the board moved to the side so they made that their destination.

'Are you sure about this Ri...dude?' Trey asked, not attempting to mask his concern.

Ricky didn't feel like dignifying the remark with an answer. Who the fuck Trey thought he was these days was becoming a very annoying question. He continued walking towards the stadium but didn't let on that he was scanning the area with his for any sign of an ambush.

They were both in full costume. Trey in his all black ensemble, the same balaclava he had worn for the first meeting, he hadn't been able to afford a decent piece of headwear. His guns, the pride of his collection, were positioned in the most accessible retrieval positions via the harness which had soaked up the bulk of his expenditure.

The weapons had actually come via Ricky who had used his talent to just take them from a gun store in Colorado. He had still charged Trey a hefty fee for them though.

Ricky's outfit was as crass as his name. He wore a pastel blue suit, under the jacket a crisp white shirt was open to the third button revealing a tuft of dark hair on his milky white chest. A gold chain sporting a bulky medallion with DREAM MACHINE embossed upon a gem encrusted plate hung over the black hairs. The gems were all fake. Trey wasn't sure about the chest hair.

Rather than a full head covering Ricky wore a strip that covered his eyes and nose. It was pale blue like his suit and made from polyester. As if this wasn't enough of an uninspiring look he also wore a Kevlar vest which was instantly recognisable under the snug fitting jacket.

There was no telling Ricky that he looked like a cunt.

'I know style,' The Dream Machine often said to Trey, 'no one knows style like me. I'm ahead of the fucking curve man.'

Trey was determined to let Ricky know the moment being dressed like a clown became the in-thing. But he wasn't holding his breath.

They approached the turnstile entrance. It was quiet, growing dark.

'No one here.' Trey said.

They will be inside, ass.' Ricky replied.

Trey chewed his lip. Not wanting to enter. This had Bad Guy Party Time written all over it.

'Come on you fucking faggot.' Ricky stepped forward. Trey followed, cautiously.

To their surprise the inside of the turnstile area was lit, the weak fluorescents there hidden by a wall that portioned the ticket area from the rest of the stadium. There was obviously power to the building. Trey thought this must mean that the Legion goons had been set up in here for a while. Beyond the former ticket offices, the far wall curved, following the contour of the stadium's exterior. Wide tunnels were cut at regular intervals which led to the lower seating area; in-between the tunnels were stairways to the upper floors.

There was no one to be seen.

'The fuck is this?' Ricky said, looking about nervously.

Ricky was expecting some sort of big deal welcoming party or a top dog to come over with some kind of Godfather vibe, clasp his shoulders and kiss him on each cheek. Trey thought it laughable. He also wondered how that particular style of greeting would go down with a tight-assed homophobe like Ricky.

'We should fuck this off. There's nothing I like about any of this.' Trey said, and with some force.

'No.' Ricky countered, although he didn't have the self-assuredness he had displayed earlier. 'No, they must be further in, on the track or something.'

Trey pulled out the pair of Desert Eagle pistols he kept on his hip. They were big guns, loud. You didn't have to hit the target with them to get people paying attention to you.

Ricky looked as though he was about to say something, perhaps to tell him to keep them holstered, but he didn't. He was nervous.

'Did you bring anything?' Trey asked.

Ricky shook his head. He was a lousy shot and entirely unreliable with firearms anyway. He had been fooling around with one of Trey's shotguns and almost blew his own foot off. Since then he had kept his distance.

'Ok, fuck it then.' Trey said. He didn't want to spend the rest of the evening dithering in a tunnel. He began to move forwards but bent his knees a little and turned his shoulders to present less of a profile. If anyone made the mistake of surprising him they would have a hole the size of a baseball in their head before they could shout *boo*.

The Wild Five Rapid Response Jet, 10pm

According to the company blurb and website TW6 was piloted by either Captain Courage or Dragons Claw, depending on the situation. This was a flat lie as neither man could pilot anything, but thanks to the blacked-out windows no one could see inside the cockpit and discover it was an ex-navy seal named Angelo Ayala chauffeuring the team around. All he had to do was stay in the vehicle and earn a nice retainer, so long as he didn't breach the non-disclosure agreement. And if he did he would never own his own home, car or clothes ever again. B&P lawyers scared him and most others more than any foreign combatant.

The jet could hit supersonic speed in seconds but the Suits made it very clear to Angelo that it was to cruise across the city in its hover mode. This was to allow maximum visibility, and to ensure it continued to clock up the minutes on the Pay to View. God forbid he should get to the deployment zone before the third set of advertisements had been run.

Rod sighed. In the passenger area, the team chatted as though they were on a field trip. Even Chu was unusually upbeat, he smiled as one of the girls made some remark to him. Rod didn't hear what it was. His mind was too busy with thoughts he was struggling to marshal. The noise in his head was like a river roaring past his ears.

He needed a drink. Something was wrong with all of this. He really needed a drink.

'Six months of nothing and then SLAM, name, address, social security number.' It tore at his reason. There was nothing right about that whatsoever. 'Who would keep a file on these guys, who was watching them, why would they just hand over the intel? They could have scored hundreds of thousands of dollars off Bartlett & Pearce in reward money.' None of it was right. He really, really needed a drink.

Biohazard Quarantine and Containment Facility, Prof Nils Study, 10pm

Nils didn't feel comfortable with Carver sat next to him. The Commander was built like a linebacker and seemed to *loom*. He wondered if he might be Enhanced, but the powers that be appeared to have some resistance to putting them in positions of power. Especially when investigating their own kind. This made sense to Nils, he wouldn't like some telepath or other person gifted in mind-fucking powers looking over his shoulder. They wouldn't even need to look over his shoulder, the shoulder would be entirely optional. He grimaced.

'*Fucking Enhanced.*' he thought

On his main monitor TW6 was moving slowly over the skyline and Carver had brought up the stream of Cell 12 to a separate screen. Nils glanced at it every minute to see if the thing had changed position. He was feeling slightly pensive. He expected to look up at some point and suddenly see it staring at him with those baleful eyes, like in a horror movie.

Carver produced his own pad, a smaller pocket device than the one Nils used at his desk. He flicked through registration reports on The Wild Five. Then stopped and turned to Nils.

'How did Raynes end up as leader of this team? According to these evaluations the man is a mental train wreck.'

Nils shrugged. 'I don't know. He looks the part I suppose. He's got the build. Those flinty blue eyes that make the ladies go all weak at the knees, floppy blond hair. The republican neo-Nazi's love that combo, and he can fly, of a fashion.'

Carver didn't care for Nils's strange attitude. The man was in his fifties, had more letters after his name than you would find on a scrabble board and appeared to have a grasp on physics, chemistry and biology that should have made him one of the world's most renowned scientists. Instead he managed to do nothing other than create debts for himself, vast debts across the globe and had subsequently ended up as another bitch for the government.

Nils's contract meant he couldn't leave the facility for three years. This the Professor never failed to complain about. Not gripping Nils's throat and squeezing it until his eyes popped out was a test of Carver's willpower and resolve. The man was infuriating to the extent that he had once had the professor confined to his quarters for a month. To keep him safe.

But when the department was faced with a problem like the thing in Cell 12 Nils could be invaluable. He was lousy with people but with numbers, probabilities and determining outcomes he was impressive. Kept under pressure and close observation the Professor got things done. Take that pressure off and there was no lazier man in the universe. He would binge on TV shows and sleep for inordinate amounts of time. When awake he played computer games, although anything that allowed contact with other players was disabled.

'These corporations are reckless. They are playing with fire,' Carver said, but Nils wasn't listening. Instead the Professor patted his arm excitedly.

'Look, the engines are firing up, they must be ready to go.'

Carver turned his attention to the screen. The engines of TW6 had indeed begun to glow with an orange heat. He took another sidelong glance at Nils, who was almost grinning as he watched the jet power off into the distance, his attitude had gone from almost total disinterest to popcorn munching fascination.

'You are very odd individual,' Carver thought, and returned his attention to the live stream.

The West Coast Olympic Stadium, 10:04 pm

Trey halted at the tunnel exit. It led out to the lower seating area at roughly the middle of the east side of the stadium. The massive floodlights, all functioning, illuminated the thousands of weather-beaten seats. The open roof of the stadium could close in the event of poor weather and he wondered why it had not been shut when the Olympic events had finished.

'Probably doesn't work now', he thought.

He looked back to Ricky who was walking very slowly towards him. His usual bravado had drained out of him. The strip of polyester across his eyes couldn't hide his nervousness.

It was as he looked back at Ricky that Trey noticed for the first time that graffiti was painted all along the walls of the tunnel. He had been so focused on looking at what was ahead that he had completely missed it. It was strange. Not the usual colorful tags or stylized art. The walls were covered in shapes.

'They look like those Viking things,' he thought.

He had seen them on a documentary about the European raiders of the dark ages. The word came to his mind, *'Runes.'*

He looked out towards the center of the stadium and could see figures moving towards it from the far side.

'Ri… Dude!' he called to Ricky, who stopped.

Trey waved him to come forward. Ricky remained motionless.

'What is it?

'Your guys, they are here.' Trey said.

'They're not *my guys*,' Ricky said sharply. 'What do they want?'

'How the fuck do I know? They are in the middle of the track.' Trey pointed and Ricky finally sidled up to him.

'What do we do? Do we go to them?' Ricky asked, he intended abandoning all responsibility from here on.

'I don't know. I guess so. They said we were to meet them here so…'

'Right.' Ricky still didn't make any motion to move into the open.

Trey puffed. He wanted this to be over. He wanted Ricky to man up and finish what he had started. This was his big fucking deal after all.

'Fuck it. Let's leave then.' Trey said.

'No! Wait. We can't just leave. They'll be pissed.' Ricky said, alarmed.

'So what, they don't know us.'

Ricky was silent.

'Dude, did you tell these fucking guys anything about us.'

Ricky's lips quivered a little, as though he was about to speak but the words hadn't reached his mouth just yet.

A voice boomed over the loudspeaker system.

'PLEASE. COME TO THE MIDDLE OF THE ARENA. YOU ARE SAFE.'

'Well, there's our invitation.' Trey said, 'Dude I hope you haven't fucked us.'

Ricky bristled. Feeling that the situation was regaining some stability his confidence returned a little.

'Don't fucking talk to me like that. I told them fuck all. People do what I say, not the other way around.'

Trey decided to ignore him. He wasn't going to engage with Ricky's bullshit while they were in the middle of a situation he didn't have handle on.

—

56

He moved away from the tunnel, made his way down the aisle and towards the track running around the outside of the arena.

'Hey!' Ricky protested, then quickly stepped up to Trey's side.

Having realized he had missed the graffiti in the tunnel because he was concentrating on one direction Trey was more alert to his surroundings as he walked. There were more of the symbols. They had been painted all around the advertising boards edging the track.

There were only three of the men in cowls at the center. Trey thought two of them were the same guys who had spoken to them outside but he couldn't be sure. He and Ricky crossed all of the lanes of the track and closed in on them.

Trey wasn't sure if maybe he had some kind of Enhanced danger sense but every fiber of his being told him that this was not what it seemed.

'For the record, I don't like this.' Trey said.

'Shut the fuck up *Sightmaster*,' Ricky sneered, 'Leave this to me.'

The three men each raised their right hand as Ricky and Trey moved within speaking distance.

'Welcome Dream Machine, welcome Sightmaster,' the one in the middle, Trey thought it must be Lefty, said with a smile, 'Legion opens its arms and embraces you.'

'I wouldn't do that to Dream Machine if I were you guys, he's touchy about that kind of thing.' Trey said, surprising himself at his boldness in mocking Ricky so blatantly.

Ricky shot him a furious look but was point blank ignored, but feeling emboldened by the greeting he stepped forward.

'Look, I'm the fucking organ grinder here OK, don't get distracted by the performing sidekick.'

Had he been more attentive to Ricky's comments Trey would have been angry at being dismissed as nothing more than his bitch, but something else had caught his eye.

There was a good deal of trash about the floor of the arena, including sections of broken and rotting stage, benches and even hurdles that had once been jumped by people with actual human sporting ability. But some areas had been cleared and Trey could see the same symbols, or similar ones, painted onto the floor. He held back as Ricky walked up to the three and began to talk to them.

He looked up at the open roof. Stars were beginning to twinkle in the sky. He peered around the stadium. At least one other person was here because the announcement would have come from the observation booth at the North end. He looked down towards the lower seating once again

He saw figures.

He guessed they had emerged from the tunnels but they could also have been crouching down behind the advertising boards. He turned and took in the whole arena. There were people spaced evenly about it the perimeter. There was something else too, each was carrying something. Something tall, slightly reflective. Like... a window pane, but narrow.

His asshole partner was apparently in deep discussion with the Legion guys, oblivious to anything going on around him.

'Uh... Machine! Can I speak to you for a second?'

'Can it *Trey*, the adults are talking.' Ricky replied, not even bothering to turn his head.

'He said my name! Fucking ASSHOLE,' Trey clenched his jaw as red thoughts clouded his mind, *'no fucking way that arrogant prick hasn't told these weird fucks everything about us,'*

He wondered if he could push Ricky with his mind. Send him flying into the Legion freaks. Move him like had done with the rock that was going to hit the dog. He tried, but there was nothing. Ricky continued to *blah blah blah* while a small army of men encircled them.

When the Wild Five Rapid Response Jet appeared above them in the huge gap of the open roof Trey thought he was probably the least surprised person in the building.

The Wild Five Rapid Response Jet, 10:10 pm

The drone cameras followed TW6 across the city. Angelo kept the vehicle at its slowest possible speed to allow their progress to be adequately covered, besides which the destination, the former Olympic Stadium was only four miles outside of the city. They could have been there in under a minute at top speed.

Rod came up front to the cockpit and took the empty co-pilots seat.

'You won't be sat long Captain, the LZ is just ahead.' Angelo said.

Rod looked out into the twilight and could see the enormous oval domed structure. A strong glow was emanating from the top.

'The roof is still open.' he said.

'Yes sir.' Angelo replied. 'I can drop this baby right down inside if it's clear. What do you think?'

Rod nodded. 'Yes, that should be fine, we can deploy Bots once we are on the ground.'

'Roger that.' Angelo said and positioned the crafts engines for a vertical descent.

Rod decided to stay up front for this last part of the approach. He would get a good look at the landing area and besides, he didn't feel in the mood for listening to the others talk about charity gigs, complimentary hotel stays and company bonuses.

As TW6 arrived over the gaping roof and began to slowly descend into the stadium Rod looked under the craft via an external camera. The surface was littered with debris, but it was nothing the jets landing gear couldn't handle.

There was a group of people in the very middle as well, not just the two they expected, and this concerned him. Were Trey Storno and Ricky Mayweather part of a larger group? Something else touched at his senses. It was probably difficult to discern from the ground but up here it was obvious to him that the trash and filth had been cleared to make concentric bands of circles and within these bands were strange rune-like shapes. Like a magic circle.

Biohazard Quarantine and Contain... You know where this is by now. Prof Nils Study. 10:10pm

'That's a magic circle!' Nils said, sitting upright and pointing at the monitor.

'Are you sure?' Carver said, the image had moved from a bottom view, seen from the undercarriage of TW6, to a drone's eye view of the top as it descended.

'Of course I'm sure.' Nils replied. 'What else looks like a magic circle?'

'What does it mean?' Carver asked, he also leaned forward.

'How should I know? I'm a research scientist, not Aleister fucking Crowley.' Nils replied.

'Well find someone who does.' Carver growled. 'If you are research scientist start *researching.*'

Nils pulled a face worthy of any teenager denied an afternoon at the mall with his buddies. He didn't want to miss the show. He tapped at his pad.

'If we hadn't screwed over the Witch this would be a lot easier.'

'Just get me the answer Nils.' Carver snapped.

TW6 was descending slowly into the stadium. B&P Drones danced around the jet, offering various angles of vision for their subscribers.

'Press the blue button until you get the best shot of it please.' Nils said.

'What?'

'The remote. Keep pressing the blue button, it will cycle through the drones. I need a clear shot of the circle.'

Carver picked up the monitors remote and did as instructed. He came to a bird's eye view of the ground from a Drone designated SkyEye 9.

'Got it.' Carver advised.

He watched as the Professor lifted his pad and took a photo of the screen. Nils then tapped a few virtual buttons and a *whoosh* sound followed as the encrypted image was sent into the web.

'I don't know how quickly we will get an answer for this.' Nils said.

Carver nodded. 'Just make sure it can't be traced back to us.'

'Of course,' Nils replied, as he continued to paw at the pad. 'I know what I'm doing.'

Carver returned his attention to the monitor. The people who had been gathered in the middle of the arena had scattered. He pressed the blue button to skip through the drone views. Something else had caught his attention.

'There are others in there. Around the perimeter of the track.'

Nils looked up. 'It's party time then,' he said, practically rubbing his hands.

'Ambush!' One of the Legion men shouted. Trey wasn't sure which one as his whole attention had been drawn to the graceful entrance into the stadium of the Wild Five jet.

'Gentlemen, you must move, prepare to defend yourselves!' one of the Legion goons shouted.

It seemed like a good idea though and Trey immediately bolted for cover. Ricky didn't appear to have caught up with the situation and stood, staring upwards.

'Fucks sake Ricky, *MOVE!*' Trey shouted. He didn't give a fuck about using real names now. Shit had just got serious.

Ricky seemed to wobble for a moment then began to run away from the centre, looking for an exit, he had no intention of remaining in the stadium.

'RICKY, COME TO ME,' Trey shouted, the volume of the jets thrusters was surprisingly low and he knew Ricky would be able to hear him. But the Dream Machine kept running.

'*Asshole.*' Trey thought.

There was no way on earth this could end with them just strolling out the way they had come in. No amount of wish thinking in the world was going to make that a reality. There would be guards in the tunnels, or barricades or a cordon of police around the building, something would be there to ensure that whatever was going to happen, happened right here.

While the noise of TW6's thrusters wasn't deafening the force of the air it pushed into the ground to enable its descent blasted a cloud of dust across the arena. Trey ducked behind a collapsed portion of a stage and closed his eyes to prevent the particles from blinding him. Within seconds the jet settled onto the ground and the engines died down.

Trey listened carefully. Not daring to look above his cover. He carefully holstered his Desert Eagles and pulled the M23 Assault Rifle from the clips across his back. He would need to suppress them. The chances of him getting a clear shot as the heroes deployed was small if these guys knew what they were doing. He glanced around to see if there was any sign of Ricky, careful not to rise above his cover. His partner was nowhere to be seen.

'Left me here, just took off. Cowardly fuck.' Trey thought as he checked his magazine. *'If I could see you, if I could just see you right now, I'd kill you,'* he thought, and knew he meant it.

'We are secure on the ground Captain and Bots are ready to roll.' Angelo said. 'Scans report no one in the area, looks like they bolted'

Rod rose from the co-pilots seat.

'Thank you Lieutenant,' Rod said, as he prepared to walk back to the passenger area. It was time for the duck hunt.

He paused, then turned to face the pilot.

'Wait, no one? I saw five people with my own eyes, right in the middle of the arena, and possibly more on the outside edge.'

'Scans show no one in the building now Sir.'

Rod shook his head, 'There's not much chance they all moved out so quickly. That means our systems are being blocked.'

Angelo tapped onto his HUD and fired off another round of detection waves.

'Everything is reporting fine Captain. They could have fled, escaped through the tunnels to the exits.'

'No, no they couldn't,' Rod replied, 'I have that covered.' He left the cockpit.

What should follow now ran through his thoughts, it was simple and well-rehearsed. The sensor array on TW6 would locate and identify all enemy units. A half dozen Assault Bots would disengage from the craft's hull and the things, which looked like garbage cans on mechanical spider legs, would seek out their targets and deliver a withering barrage of large calibre rounds. After the bad guys had been softened up, or possibly killed, he would lead the team in carefully choreographed exit from the craft.

Rod had doubts about this. Something wasn't right.

As he entered the passenger area the team were checking their costumes were fitted correctly. The ladies looked like goddesses in their skin-tight suits, Chu had on what looked like a modern take on the robes of some ancient Emperor, he often complained that he could barely move in them, but B&P insisted he wear them for 'A List' missions. Hyper-ton, who looked like three men welded together, only wore leggings and a redundant vest, it was stretched across his ridiculously muscle bound body only to carry the new team colours.

'We will be disembarking in just a second.' Rod said. He pulled his cell phone out of a pocket and hit speed dial.

———

66

'Alex, can you hear me all right?' Rod asked, as the line connected, he was sure he could hear the wind rushing past the phone as Alex blasted around the stadium.

'Sure buddy. You done already?' Alex replied.

'Just about to start. Listen have you seen anyone come out of the building, any of the exits opened up?'

'Not a soul. There is an open exit on the west side but no one has come through it. I'm completing a circuit of this place about every five seconds. If anyone leaves, I'll see them.'

'Ok buddy. Thanks again for doing this.' Rod said.

'No problem Rod, a pleasure.' Alex replied, and as he passed the open door of the west entrance he slowed a little to make sure that all was as it should be, then sped up and began to phase in and out of the world again.

'You talking to that fucking faggot?' Hyper-ton said with his usual unbridled aggression.

'Can it Frank.' Chu said.

'Fuck you Kung Fu. This is supposed to be a Wild Five show, not a fucking Gay Pride event.'

'Jesus Frank.' Vanessa said shaking her head.

'What? You think it's right Captain Jim Beam over there gets to bring along any fucking asshole he likes? That could fuck up our contracts.'

'No one's contract is at risk Frank.' Rod said calmly, 'Alex is just helping out because I asked him too. He's not after a piece of your bonus or your bigoted, ignorant redneck ass, OK?'

Hyper-ton stabbed a finger at Rod.

'You had better watch that hole of yours *Captain*, because I will have no fucking problem with pushing your teeth down it.'

'Frank, if you even breathe heavily on a member of this team while under contract to B&P, once their legal team has finished with you, you'll spend the rest of your days blowing sailors at the harbour for loose change.' Rod said, his voice still the epitome of calm and reason.

Hyper-ton made to retort. Rod raised his eyebrows and the big man remained silent.

'Good. Now team, I can't be sure but there could be a problem with our systems. We definitely had contacts on approach, but now nothing is pinging TW6's sensors now.'

'Have they run?' Chu asked.

'I don't think so. Velocity says no one has left the building. The problem is that I believe some of our sensor arrays are being jammed. Not everything, my phone works, the video stream appears to be unaffected but radar, infrared and sonar are reporting no bad guys.'

'Do you think they, the two we are after are doing it?' Fire Swan asked.

Rod could see the nervous look in her eyes, they were beautiful and wide, her mouth hung open a little after she spoke, her shoulders bunched forward as though it was cold in the comfortably heated aircraft.

'It's possible. It's also probable there are more than two of them out there. As we approached I saw what I believe was some kind meet going down below.

'Gang meet?' Chu asked.

'Again, I'm just saying it's possible. I didn't get a good look but yeah, I think they had numbers.'

'The Bots will make mincemeat of them.' Hyper-Ton said dismissively.

'Not if the Bots recon systems are also affected. In fact, I suggest we disable them anyway.' Rod said, braced for the inevitable reaction.

'Are you fucking nuts?' Hyper-Ton balked.

'I don't know Frank,' Rod said, unfazed by Hyper-Ton's temper, 'but I am fairly sure I don't want a confused, fully automated weapons platform unloading 5,000 rounds into my ass because it thinks I'm a bad guy.'

Hyper-Ton grunted.

'Look, I can't just *do* this. We're a team' Rod looked around the cabin at each of his colleagues. 'I need everyone's agreement.'

Chu nodded immediately. Phantom Lady followed, Hyper-ton moved his jaw a little, then nodded.

'Swan?' Rod asked, he regretted putting her in this position. She had only been on one other mission with them so far, a simple search and rescue in a mid-west town decimated by an F5 Tornado.

'I... I guess. Sure,' she said, looking to the others for confirmation that she was taking the right line.

Rod knew she had been promised the Bots would pretty much devastate anyone or anything that got in their way, that the TW6's on-board defence systems would protect her. He could imagine the conversation with the execs.

'All you have to do is look good honey,' they would have told her as she signed the five-year contract, 'and you are set for life. No more worries.'

Rod understood. She hadn't thought it through, she was agreeing because everyone else had, not considering that everyone else at least had experience of the danger this kind of encounter could bring. But like the repugnant spin doctors he loathed he accepted it at face value, because that gave him the outcome he wanted.

'Right, here's how it's going to go. I'll get Angelo to hold the Bots, they'll remain passive until he unblocks the signal. That way if there are any issues with him or TW6 they will kick in to gear. We go out, I'll lead followed by Chu and Hyper, ladies if you will be making sure that nothing comes at our six.'

It was sexist shit but Rod tried to sugar coat it as best as he could. Fortunately, Phantom Lady and Swan decided to buy into it without a fuss. If the men wanted to be a little 19th century in a warzone it suited them fine.

Rod rolled his eyes. 'Grab your gear, and one other thing, remember that as soon as we exit the B&P drones will be watching us. Poses, heroic looks, flex a little. You know the score.'

They all nodded, then set about selecting their weapons. Rod looked at his phone. There was nothing from Alex. He walked back a little and called to Angelo.

'Lieutenant, I need you to switch the Bots too passive while we investigate the area. Can't trust the surveillance right now.

'Roger that Captain.' Angelo replied.

'Okay ramblers, let's get rambling.' Rod said, turned to the side of the craft and pushed engaged the release handle for the side door.

It slid quickly and quietly open, a small ramp had already extended down to the floor. He moved quickly through the door, above him two B&P drones flitted about, capturing the best view of the heroes as they disembarked. As the door had opened Rod heard a voice, talking, it was coming over the loudspeaker.

'Not talking', he corrected himself, it was more rhythmic, as though he were reciting poetry. There was also a kind of low key chant coming from all around him.

He peered into the stadium, the dust cloud had thinned considerably and thanks to his enhanced vision he could make out the array of people on the edge of the stadium. They all appeared to have something in front of them, like narrow windows.

'*Riot shields?*' Rod thought.

Chu appeared at his side. He had leapt down from the jet and rolled into position, he slid a katana from its scabbard. The fans loved that sort of thing.

Hyper-Ton came down next. In his hands he gripped a huge two-handed hammer. It looked as though it had been forged by dwarves and handed down through the centuries, but was in fact one of a dozen or so mass produced by B&P. The hammerhead contained an explosive charge that could be detonated by a vocal command from Hyper-Ton. He got through one each mission and the public just assumed the hammer was magical and somehow survived the blast.

Phantom Lady did her handsprings. Basic stuff, she had no real skill in martial arts or was even particularly athletic. Beneficial genetics and a rigorous cardio routine with Philippe, the team's physical exercise coach was what kept her body looking smoking hot. Finally, Swan appeared. The choreographer had trained her to walk to the ramp, place her hands on her hips and look slightly up, then she was to put her hands forwards and ignite them.

Rod recalled observing the routine as she was instructed in the gym.

'Biiiig Circles then darling. Big Circles,' the lithe little Latino man called as he pranced around, 'Stretch those arms. Let the people see those glorious flames and then...' the choreographer performed a pirouette, 'spin down to the bottom and join the others.'

She did none of this. She peered out through the doorway. Plainly terrified. He was tempted to tell her to hold back, to *protect the jet*, or something, but at this moment he was reminded that radio communications were still functioning. The voice of Eddie Banes rasped into his ear.

'Raynes! Get that dumb cunt off that plane.'

'Yes Sir.' Rod replied. He held out a hand towards Swan.

'It's OK, come over to me.' he said.

But it wasn't OK. It was then that the rockets, from six different sections of the arena, were launched at TW6.

Trey considered his options, but they were few. First on the list was to start firing, just blast his way back towards the tunnel they had entered by. The Legion guys had acted as though this was all a huge surprise, that they were trying to protect him and Ricky, but he knew *absolutely* that was bullshit. This was a set-up. As sure as shit. These weird assholes had brought them here for specifically for this.

Whether it was for a bounty, or they worked for the government and were bringing in unregistered Enhanced he wasn't sure, but something told him the fruit loops weren't holding hands with The Wild Five or Bartlett & Pearce. No, this was something else.

But the the situation called for action and action right now. He still had no clue where Ricky was and he needed to make his mind up soon because things were unlikely to get any easier once a bunch of Enhanced appeared out of their super jet.

Over the loudspeaker, a voice began to talk as if in prayer and in a language entirely foreign to him. He thought it might well be the same person who had advised them they were safe when they had arrived.

'*What the fuck?*' Trey thought.

Around him the sound of dozens of other people sounded, chanting he thought, a low hum began to chorus around the stadium.

From the sides of the jet several mechanical gun turrets had scuttled into position around it. Trey had expected them to open fire or at least do something but instead they just stood still, silent and threatening.

'This is getting better every minute,' Trey said as he released the safety on his weapon, decision made.

He would head for the tunnel. Unload a clip into his path to keep the assholes down and then switch to his pistols for close-up work. It wasn't a great plan but it was a serviceable plan. It was Plan A. Plan B would be to stay here and shoot until he was shot or ran out of ammo and was arrested by a bunch of dick bags.

Unfortunately, as he peered above the cover of his position, he saw TW6 open its door and the one and only Captain Courage leap out of it. Ready to fight for good, to serve justice and to suck the corporate dick of Bartlett and Pearce. He was followed by the rest of the puppets, each dancing to the sound of a billion subscriptions.

'*So much for Plan A,*' he thought. He stood, brought his rifle up to his shoulder and prepared to open fire at the conveniently gathered group.

Then the world turned orange, and hot.

Same place and time. I just wanted a dramatic pause.

TW6 exploded with such force that except for Phantom Lady, whose preternatural instincts phased her body temporarily out of existence, every member of The Wild Five was thrown at least twenty feet away from where they had stood. The rockets had all struck true.

Rod had seen the missiles come streaking from the upper seating areas. He was fast, his Enhanced agility allowed him to react far quicker than any normal human being, but there was nothing he could do to help Fire Swan. He wasn't *that* fast.

He had only been able to watch as one of the rockets flashed over her head and into the open door of TW6. She had just ignited her hands and begun to wind her arms around as though she were performing ballet sequence.

The blast pushed at Rod and tossed him across the arena, and although his athletic maneuver spared him from the full impact of the explosion he landed heavily amongst a pile of disassembled timber frames. After the initial blast two more loud bangs sounded as burning debris fell about him.

'*Get to cover!*'

Rod's sense of self-preservation quickly kicked in and spoke to him urgently. From cover he could assess the situation. See who had survived the fireball. All of them had element-resistant suits so there was a chance the damage to them was reduced. Not for Fire Swan though, he was sure of that. He had seen her slender arms sliced from her body as the jet shredded, and jettisoned her into the air.

He rolled over and took in the scene. The body of the TW6 was a burning shell. A terrific volume of smoke was boiling up towards the open roof. The cockpit was also an inferno and Rod wasn't sure, but he thought the dark shadow inside it might be Angelo. A figure appeared, surprising him until he realized it was Chu,

'Captain.'

The Enhanced martial artist, called Dragons Claw because of his *featured weapon*, a titanium three-pronged claw affixed to a length of highly polished chain, extended his hand to Rod.

Then the Bots began to open fire.

'Fuck me.' Nils said. He looked up just in time to see the screen whiteout as glare from the blast overwhelmed the sensitive cameras of the drones. 'I was genuinely not expecting that. What just happened.'

Carver stared without expression at the screen.

'Rockets. I think five or six. From all sides. Every one of them hit.'

'Wow!' Nils said. 'Score one for the bad guys, I guess.'

Carver ignored the man's total lack of empathy. 'That jet was more than capable of dispersing those rockets with its countermeasures. There is no way they should have hit.'

'How can you be so sure?' Nils asked.

'We built it.' Carver replied.

Nils said nothing. Carver probably shouldn't have revealed that particular morsel of information. He decided to take it as a compliment he had been let in on the secret.

'Shit!' Nils said, excitedly pointing at the other screen. 'Did you see that?'

'Yes.' Carver said. 'Can you play it back on your pad? Double window so we can see both scenes at once.' He didn't want to lose his view of the events in the stadium.

'No problem.' Nils replied, his fingertips already tip-tapping across the screen.

He brought up the video feed and rewound it back to the moment just before TW6 became a fireball. He then added a second window on screen, the Dome Cam feed of the creature running concurrently and adjusted for the time difference.

They watched as the first screen, which displayed the young Wild Five member, Fire Swan, was washed with orange, then white as the drone's sensors were overwhelmed, at that moment the creature appeared to spasm. Its manicured fingers gripped the table edge and turned white at the knuckles. It lifted its head slightly, and both men saw its jaw clenched tightly, spittle appeared on its lips and its eyes rolled back.

'Good god.' Nils said.

'The very second the blast killed that girl.' Carver said.

'And that thing had a fucking stroke.' Nils added.

On the screen he could see the team leader, Captain Courage, getting to cover behind a large stage which was already well alight. The drones were automatically keeping their distance until their sensors told them it was safer to move back in.

The picture began to become clear once again. Carver clicked through the drones until he found one which was still close enough to get a good view of the scene.

'I thought there was a delay on these live broadcasts? To stop stuff like this being seen.' Nils said.

'Not for us.' Carver replied.

'Do Bartlett and Pearce know that?'

Carver gave Nils a sidelong glance and said nothing.

'Right.' Nils gave a nod. Today truly was a day of sharing.

The theme tune to the Benny Hill Show suddenly burst from Nil's pad.

Carver stared hard at him.

'It's an email from Dr. Nevatte at MIT. She's replying about the circle.' Nils said

'That's inappropriate Nils.' Carver said sharply, 'get it changed.'

'Right.' Nils said, with no intention of doing so.

'What does she say?' Carver asked, he had returned his gaze to the monitor, there was movement in the stadium.

'Uhm,' Nils said, as he skimmed through the body of the communication. 'Well, she says it's definitely a work of occult rites. That it appears to be some form of containing circle. And that...' Nils stopped and looked up, 'am I missing anything?'

'No.' Carver said. 'Get on with it.'

Nils took a quick look at the monitor, he could see Dragons Claw stood over Captain Courage offering a hand up. He returned to the email.

'She says there are a lot of symbols in it which are unknown to her but it's hard to say because the picture isn't great... saucy bitch, everyone's a fucking critic...'

'Nils!' Carver warned.

'She says from what she can make out the elements that are recognizable point to it being part of a ritual of sacrifice.'

'Sacrifice.' Carver said, something with a cold hand reached into his memories and stirred them.

'Apparently.' Nils replied. 'She says it's an incredibly big circle and asks if are we sacrificing the Hanks Bay Steamrollers Football Team.' Nils frowned. 'I think she's joking about that.'

Carver leaned forward and took the remote to Nils second monitor. He expanded the image of Cell 12. The creature had still not moved. It remained with its head bowed, hands and arms splayed.

'I think she's closer to the truth of it than she knows.' Carver grimly.

'What do you mean?'

'I think there is a connection here.'

'Here?'

'With him. With that.'

Nils looked at the creature. It didn't take long for him to take up the Commanders train of thought and add it to his own. The vast repository of his mind began to collate information at the speed of his genius intellect.

It was all about numbers, quantity, and quality. Enhanced heroes were killed every week but not the very powerful. By definition the greater their ability the more difficult they were to kill by intent or chance. But the lesser ones, who often formed small groups of vigilantes, had been suffering of late. Occasionally it was straight up murder, a hit by a revenging mob boss or just some lunatic with a machete and a set of skewed principles. Then there were the accidents and the massacres. An accident like the team that was called to rescue children who had found themselves stuck deep inside an abandoned steel works. Before they could locate the children, there had been an explosion.

The bodies were never recovered. Digging up thousands of tons of metal to get to some very dead Enhanced heroes and a couple of dumb kids was never going to happen. It was put down to a gas pocket igniting. The investigation probably lasted as long as it took to find paperclips for the files.

Then there were cases like that of Magnifique Etalons, the French team he had looked at today. For them it was the abandoned water treatment plant. That time it was not so subtle, an ambush had taken them down, but the result was the same, a bunch of dead Enhanced all in the same place.

'And now here we are in an abandoned Olympic stadium, with a collection of superheroes and couple of villains who just had a jet explode in their faces, all right on top of a circle designed to receive sacrifices.'

Nils mind moved at speed through the options. All of the pertinent data was summoned and arranged in all possible outcomes.

'Christ, its fucking Wicker Man,' he said.

'What do you mean Nils.' Carver asked, 'what's going on.

'She was sacrificed to it. The circle, that's where they have to do it. I'll bet they have to enter it willingly or some other such horseshit but yes, that's what we just saw, a sacrifice to that thing in there.'

'How sure are you?' Carver asked. The question carried the inference that the answer was going to lead to a grave decision.

'I'm as certain as I can be given the evidence I've seen. This isn't the first group to be taken out like this, although this is… almost theatrical in its operation, they must have known that the whole thing would be televised.'

'Meaning?' Carver demanded.

'They wanted people to see this. There is a message here I think.'

Carver nodded.

Nils returned to the scene at the stadium. The drones were moving back in to a better vantage point having determined that the risk was now manageable.

It took Carver a moment to realize that the streaks on the screen were not distortions in the video feedback but the illuminated trails of tracer rounds being fired into the arena.

The explosion took Trey off his feet and threw him backwards. There was nothing to cushion his fall and he tumbled over, various parts of his guns jabbed at his back and side.

It hurt.

'Fuck!'

He blinked and took a deep breath of heated air. Something made a '*dunk*' noise to his left. Then *thwock, thwock, thwock*. Debris. Pieces of the jet were falling.

'Jesus.'

A flaming shard of fuselage appeared from the dark cloud that boiled above him. It was going to slice him in half.

Trey *caught* it. He saw himself, staring upwards, arms splayed out to the sides. Time didn't slow down, he was sure of that, instead his mind was moving too fast for it to keep up. He nudged his ride a little and the flaming panel changed course.

'*At my feet, it will be cover.*' Trey thought.

The shard turned a little, a graceful arc. Trey let it go. It slammed into the ground two feet below his feet creating a flaming wall that hid him from anyone still alive near the billion-dollar bonfire that had once been TW6.

'Holy shit.' Trey said.

He sat up, ignoring the dull pain in his bruised back. The piece of wreckage had planted itself at least a foot into the floor.

'*Fluke,*' he thought. '*I couldn't have done that.*'

He realized his rifle was gone. Lost when the blast took him. He pulled out a Desert Eagle and got to his feet but kept low. Dust and smoke filled the arena. Trey checked behind him first but could see no one coming towards him, nor anyone in the seating due to the obfuscation cloud.

'*If I can't see they them hopefully they can't see me.*'

He peered around the fuselage, careful not to touch its red hot edges. What was left of the jet boiled with flames. It was sat within a pool of fire where its fuel had splashed.

'*That's going to need a new paint job.*' he thought and pulled out his second Desert Eagle. He deliberately avoided thinking about what has just happened, it would slow him down.

He saw movement. Something or someone big was moving ahead, beyond the jet. The heat distorted the air far too much for him to see clearly. Suddenly he was under fire. Rounds smashed into the fuselage, around him, above him. It was wild fire and it was coming from the jet.

'Whoo fuck,' Trey yelped as he ducked back behind his protective piece of TW6.

He could tell the rounds were large caliber, they were almost penetrating the resistant skin of the jets panel. The fire was constant.

'Gotta be the Bots.'

He thought he might have heard a few screams and shouts. Away from the center.

'Legion guys getting tagged. Those things they were carrying looked like riot shields. Large caliber rounds will chew them up like candy.'

Trey knew the Bots had limited ammunition. They were there to soften up a target before the troops rolled in.

'I'll bet their sensors and programming have taken a shit. Just got to sit it out until they eat through their supply.'

He crouched. No point moving. The bullets were being fired with no thought as to where they were going to impact so everyone was as much a target as he was.

'Go ahead, *do your thing little robotwots.'*

The panel bucked from the impact of so many rounds but didn't appear to be ready to let any through. Satisfied he was safe from anyone on the other side of his cover Trey returned his attention to the stadium seating.

He heard another scream. This was louder, possibly closer.

'Moving on me. Brave or stupid.'

Trey pulled back the hammers on each pistol. He considered switching to his shotgun but decided it would be better suited if they got *real* close.'

At last, a figure emerged from the gloom. Trey didn't wait long enough to identify his target. There was no point. It was pretty clear that everything in here with him was an enemy, and in the remote possibility that they weren't he could soon fix that.

He fired. The Eagle ion his right hand boomed against the noise of the fire and the blurred figure dropped. Another appeared, another cannon blast, this one from his left hand to keep the clips even, the second figure joined his colleague.

They were simple shots. Mr. Magoo would struggle to miss at this range, even with the distorting effect of hot air and smoke. Trey felt nothing odd. No sensation of being *with* the bullet as they left the chamber despite his odd desire for it to be just like that.

Then they came in number. The first two had obviously been sent to determine his location. Willing victims? Trey remained crouched to present less of a profile, he raised both guns, arms out, and slightly bent to allow for the recoil the mighty Eagles produced.

'I never miss,' he thought.

But he never missed a *single target*, he used a rifle, inherently better suited to hitting the mark than a pistol, he had a good quality scope, although he did feel he had never really needed it. Would his ability work for him in this situation? With multiple enemies to track?

'WELCOME TO THE TRIAL RUN BOYS,' Trey shouted, and began to rhythmically squeeze the triggers of his Eagles.

Trey was *with* each round before it left its barrel. His vision opened up in to six unique perspectives. He could see, from each bullet, its direction and its target. He guided each one with a gentle nudge or tweak to the precise location he wished it to penetrate.

'Head shots,' he thought.

His guess as to what the narrows windows had been proved to be correct, two of the Legion people carried riot shields, no doubt to counter both the debris from the jet they were going to blow up and any subsequent gunfire from himself, after all if they knew of him, which they clearly did, then they knew it was his forte.

The shields presented no problem. He guided two of the bullets in a grand arc, crossing the path of their brothers and then brought them around to the rear of his targets. He was both able to maintain the speed of those headed to the men without shields and also the velocity of those on the more protracted journey. His goal was simple. He wanted the bullets all to hit at the same time. Mostly for effect.

'I wonder if this is how a spider sees with all those eyes' he thought, as he choreographed his ballet of bullets.

Blood and brains spattered against the riot shields. Each of the Legion men dropped simultaneously as their heads were burst open by the enormous kinetic energy of the .357 caliber rounds.

'Booyah.' Trey thought. Things had just gotten interesting. *'I can do this shit. This is what I do! I don't just aim the fucking bullets I AM THE FUCKING BULLETS!'*

More Legion pressed forwards. Trey fired into them. This time he only used one shot and took it on a journey, experimenting with his revealed talent. After all, if he was going to die he wanted to go to Hell, or whatever awaited him when these assholes overwhelmed him, with at least some idea of what he had missed out on.

He weaved the shot in and out of the chests of the oncoming attackers as though he were stitching a seam. The round smashed bones, ruptured organs and tore skin away from their backs. Eight people died from the single bullet. It shouldn't have done. Their muscle should have degraded both the physical body of the round and its speed.

'This puts that JFK thing into a whole new perspective.' Trey thought.

Another bang issued from behind the panel. Some protected thing on the jet had finally given in to the heat. Trey holstered one of his Eagles and picked up a piece of rubble, about the same size as the chunk Ricky had thrown at the dog.

He waited for another attacker. Three came striding towards him. He tossed the rock into the air as though he was about to strike it like a baseball.

Nothing happened. The rock dropped to the floor as physics intended.

'Oh.' he thought.

The Legion men charged. They were carrying long wicked looking knives. Trey focused on the knives. Tried to move them, twist them from their owner's hands. They remained gripped with homicidal strength.

'Shit,' he said.

He let his Eagle do the talking and blasted each man in the chest, the shots unaided by his ability.

A terrific volley of gunfire sounded from behind the panel. Not the twotbots this time but it was still automatic fire and it was incoming.

'I guess some of the Five are still walking,' he thought.

He holstered the pistol and retrieved his shotgun from his back. He desperately wanted to see what was going on around the jet. Mindful of what might be coming at him from the smoke cloud he peered around the fuselage.

The smoke was just as dense but through it streaks of light zipped along from the seating area.

'Tracer rounds.'

They were narrowing in on a spot directly ahead of him, about twenty feet beyond what was left of TW6. *'Must be where the good guys are.'*

He pulled off his balaclava. It was too hot. *'Fuck it if they see me.'*

Trey stayed low and began to move into the storm.

Thanks to her ability Vanessa had a sixth sense where danger to herself was concerned. She had read that a lot of Enhanced had this sharpened instinct for self-preservation. She had, what the egg heads termed, *de-constructed*, probably less than a second before the jet exploded.

She didn't understand any of it. Before The Wild Five she had been a working mom, waiting-on at a roadside diner on the I32 out of Hanks Bay. God had given her a pretty face, a killer ass and parents who couldn't afford her college.

She had tried to live a real person's life. She had worked all of the hours available and with two jobs for a while, building the cash up to get at least some sort of adult schooling, but then she had met Denny one summer.

A sweet-talking guy with a mess of dark hair and a perfect smile. He talked how she thought a poet might. He observed the human condition, and nature, and how both might be seen through the eyes of God. He never told her how beautiful she looked, as so many of the guys had when trying to gain her attention and affection, instead he told her how beautiful she *was*. That her whole being was one of patience and tolerance and love. He hadn't moved too fast. He hadn't spoiled the times they had together, when she had managed to switch shifts and get a weekend off, with clumsy attempts to fuck her in some parking lot.

Finally, lost in love and desire for him while sat on the beach during a weekend on the coast she had pulled him on top of her and they had made love as the sun dropped into the sea.

Denny was gone two weeks later. There was a note. It read,

'I have to move on V, sorry I can't be there to say goodbye but it would break my heart to do so, truly it would. So au revoir babe. Love D.

This wasn't enough. Having your heart smashed to a bloody pulp was never enough for God. She was also pregnant. A little under nine months after Denny had left his note, a baby girl who she would call Rosie after her grandma arrived, and made sure that college was something that only happened to the lucky kids. Then she had discovered she could walk through walls.

'Vanessa! Get down!' It was Rod. She could see him and Chu crouched behind a broken section of stage, some of which was on fire. It was good advice; she wasn't sure how much longer she could maintain her deconstructed form. They had tested her at the B&P research center and found her talent was unpredictable in its duration.

She moved towards them. Her body, when deconstructed, did not look too different from how she appeared normally. Rather her color shifted to a cobalt blue, even her clothes. Her ability to make her atomic structure separate, whilst maintaining a connection that kept her whole, also accommodated whatever she was wearing or holding. It was staggering, frightening, and Bartlett and Pearce were prepared to pay her five million dollars a year to show it off as part of The Wild Five.

'Rod, Christ, what's happening? Vanessa asked in a voice approaching hysteria as she knelt by her team mates. As she did so her costume regained its startling white and red hue as her body re-constructed to its natural form.

'We've been set-up, ambushed,' Rod said.

'They are all around us. Heavy ordnance.' Chu added.

'Not that they need it, we almost got killed by our own Bots. Fucking things went haywire.' Rod said.

'Where's Swan, Hyper?'

Rod shook his head. 'I don't know,' he lied. There was no need to make this any worse for Vanessa. A brief vision of Swan being lifted into the flaming air, her arms gone, ate into his thoughts.

Shots were coming from further down the arena. Not the automatic rattle of assault rifles. Single blasts, a big gun. Rod's enhanced hearing and sight guided him towards a flaming chunk of TW6.

'*Someone's enduring their own last stand down that way,*' he thought.

'Look we can't stay here. We are either going to get shot, fried or choke to death.'

'I can't stop a bullet Captain.' Chu said, I can take a lot of punishment, you know that, but a bullet will end me.'

'Yeah,' Rod nodded. 'I hear yah. We need a good old fist fight.' He turned again to Vanessa. 'Can you do your thing long enough to get out of here?

She shook her head, 'I don't know. I don't think so. Not yet at least. I was deconstructed for longer than usual, all those bullets, the fire...I... '

'It's Ok.' Rod said, 'don't worry. We will figure something out.'

As he said this Rod suddenly realized that he could hear himself think. The hail of gunfire had stopped.

'Reloading?' Chu said.

'Maybe.' Rod replied carefully, 'or maybe they are against the clock and it's taking too long to kill us.'

He risked a look above the stage. No bullets struck him or the wooden floor. He listened carefully, filtering out the noise of the fire.

'They are coming,' he said.

'Good.' Chu pulled out his second Katana, the first having been lost during the blast.

'I know you can handle yourself Vanessa, but don't take chances.'

She nodded. She looked a mess. Tears streamed down her face bringing her dark eyeliner with them.

'I can't believe I'm about to say this but I wish Hyper was here,' she said. 'God I hope Swan is OK.'

Rod could only marvel at the hope and optimism she had.

'Let's take care of us first, then we can look for the others,' he said and placed a hand on her shoulder.

She covered it with hers and rested her cheek upon it. In that moment Rod felt he could rise up and take on the whole lot of these maniacs himself. Passion and longing surged through his body.

'Raynes... Raynes!'

It was Eddie Banes. Whatever had affected the ship must have blocked the signal into the mic affixed under his ear.

'Fuck, Rod thought. 'I should have accidentally lost this.'

'Raynes! Answer for fucks sake.'

Rod held up a hand and then tapped his ear to indicate to Vanessa and Chu that he was receiving a transmission.'

'Banes... I am receiving you now. I don't know how much of this has reached you but we have been ambushed, we have encountered heavy fire and are two members MIA.'

'Shut the fuck up Raynes. I've seen it all. I don't know how you have managed to turn this into the cluster fuck I'm staring at right now but you better your collective asses into this fight immediately.'

'Banes... we...'

'Can it asshole. You've spent enough time hiding, get out there and do what you are paid to do. All of you. You and your freaks owe me half a billion dollars in jet fighter so you better start putting on a hell of a show.'

Rod felt a fury begin to rise in him. Chu and Vanessa looked at him with expectant faces, he had to turn away.

'It's obviously skipped your attention *director* but we are in the middle of a shit storm here. Swan is dead, I repeat Swan is dead. Hyper probably the same. Do we have assistance incoming?' Rod spoke in a whispered snarl, trying to keep his voice low enough that Vanessa wouldn't hear him.

'*The police are on their way. They tend to get excited when explosions are reported.*' Banes replied.

'The police?' Rod said, incredulous. 'We need the fucking military, Enhanced, mercs, Christ I'd take the Salvation Army right now.'

'*Look Raynes, the only reason I haven't already torn up your contract is that our viewer stats just went off the fucking charts. I've got every single media hound en-route to that stadium to watch you burn, so make sure that if you do you do it with style.*'

The faint hiss that accompanied transmissions from Banes abruptly stopped. He had disconnected.

'Son of a bitch.' Rod shouted. He punched a strut under the stage and it splintered with the force.

'Rod! What's happening. Was it B&P? Are they coming for us?' Vanessa asked with fearful hope.

'CNN are coming for us V. CNN, FOX and Wild Bills Enhanced Showcase Channel, they are all coming for us.'

Vanessa turned to Chu. 'What does he mean?'

Chu rolled his shoulders and gave his Katana a deft twirl. 'He means its show business Phantom Lady. Now, let's get back to where we were.' He looked to Rod. 'I'm ready.'

'Ok,' Rod said, 'we could split, but I think we would just get swarmed. There's a lot of them. If we stick together, as a team, maybe...'

'I'm not leaving you.' Vanessa said quickly.

'*It's the fear, it's not love.*' Rod reminded himself as his heart pumped harder.

'Ok. We make for a tunnel, stay close, we fight and move, if we move fast enough we will be on top of them.'

Chu and Vanessa nodded.

He wondered how far he could fly right now. His ability came in short bursts but he had only accompanied the jet for a minute or so as it left the base. He could easily carry Vanessa, take her up with him through the open roof and out of this madness. Use the smoke as cover.

But that would leave Chu alone to face these pricks. Chu, who had never once let him down, who right now looked like some futuristic samurai ready to go full Jackie Chan on these weird assholes. Sure, he could leave and take Vanessa with him, but he wanted to fight. He wanted to give some of the pain back. And when he was done he wanted to drop the head of one these guys on Banes desk, unzip his fly, get his Captain Courage Cock out, and piss on it.

'Let's go,' Rod said.

Trey moved as fast as he could back towards the jet. No one appeared to be following him.

'*They gave up quickly.*'

The thought didn't sit well with him. These guys were clearly zealots. Zealots with a serious arsenal, yet they had come at him with knives.

'*Why didn't they just shoot me?*'

92

It puzzled him, and as he edged closer he realised that the shooting had stopped ahead of him too. He peered into the haze. There were figures, a fight was going on towards the edge of the track, over the advertising boards. The Wild Five were now on the offensive.

'Why the fuck is Legion fighting these guys toe to toe... they have fucking assault rifles and rocket launchers.'

He looked behind him, still no one appeared to be following.

Every fibre of Treys being told him that this was not good.

'What *is* your game assholes,' he called out.

'They could probably get a shot off at me here. I've no cover, if they just sprayed the area there's a good chance I'd be winged at the very least.'

He looked around. He looked up at the vortex of flame and thick oily smoke rising through the roof, he took in every possible piece of cover available to him, he looked at the floor and saw a symbol painted onto it.

He then studied all of this more carefully.

'It's been cleared,' he thought.

The turf had been swept of dust and debris and a small patch was left clear, for a symbol to be painted onto it. He looked about for more areas like this. He saw others. Then he saw the circle.

About eight feet away in the direction he was headed he could see the path that followed the curve of a circle had been cleared, just like the patch right by him. Inside two thick bands with strange designs between them ran as far as he could see.

'What the fuck is that?

Trey thought quickly. The shooting and the assaults had stopped as he began to move back this way, towards the team of heroes he had thought, but perhaps it had stopped because he was moving towards this strange circle.

'*Am I being herded this way by you fuckers?*'

He bristled at the thought he was being manipulated but he had little choice in the matter. Besides, he wanted to go out fighting B&P sponsored assholes not some pasty-faced religious fucktards.

He continued towards the melee that was going on ahead.

As Rod and the team broke cover shots immediately rang out. Bullets thudded into the stage and around their feet but none struck them.

'*Lousy shots.*' Rod thought, '*lucky us.*'

As they moved further forward he picked up on a group approaching. There was a good number of them.

'Here they come!' he shouted.

Chu lifted his katana above his head, ready to strike. Vanessa tried to keep behind Rod, she could fight, in a basic way, she had been shown a few martial arts moves and boxed every day. She enjoyed the rigorous training exercise and B&P had even allowed Rosie to take part in some of the sessions, but she was not a natural fighter. Her role had been to take the viewers breath away as she walked through walls and locked doors, to reach through solid windows and unlock vehicles.

In the aftermath of the earthquake they had flown out to she had been able to reach victims trapped under rubble and hand them parcels of food and bottles of water. It had been wonderful, uplifting.

She also knew Rod was in love with her. It would be obvious to any woman, and he treated her with kindness and respect and in truth he was a good-looking man for his age. But she didn't feel that way about him. She knew she was guilty of playing to his feelings, keeping him on her side, but what other choice did she have?

When the first group attacked, she stepped back and prepared to deconstruct. Rod and Chu would have to deal with this. It was their thing. They didn't have a daughter to go home to. The fact of the matter was that Chu was a childless vengeful widower and Rod a middle-aged alcoholic divorcee. They had a reason to die, only she had a reason to live.

Rod charged into the group as they came forwards. Each man was dressed in a cowl fashioned from a dull brown material. Each carried a long knife, which they held in front of them threateningly.

'These guys have no fucking clue how to fight with a knife.' Rod thought.

This proved to be correct.

As he closed in he heard the *whoosh* of Chu's Katana as he began to carve through people at the front and side of him. For his part he simply leaned in a little, prompting the knife-wielding villains to attempt to slash at him, it was almost too easy. As they missed, Rod had feinted the lean forward, he leapt up and into them and delivered a series of staggeringly powerful blows.

He went for the head of each man with punches that struck like a jackhammer. Fragile skulls shattered and jaws were broken in two. The concussion of one blow forced an eyeball out of his victim's head.

Rod began to feel his adrenalin rise, as though it were a superheated flow of energy. His hands and legs became whirring, punishing weapons of violence. Rather than diminishing as he piled into the crowd of attackers his strength ramped up. He was able to toss their bodies into the air as though they were nothing but sacks of wet sponge.

But more came. The stream of attackers seemed endless and Rod began to lose ground. They were being pushed back and it was difficult keeping upright as they stumbled over bodies they had already deposited to the floor.

Rod looked back to Vanessa, she was backing away, towards the jet.

'Vanessa! Rod shouted above the clamour of the battle, 'stay with us.'

She shook her head.

'Christ!' Rod snarled. He snatched up a man from the floor by his legs and began to swing him into his colleagues like a club.

'Chu, we have to fall back, Vanessa is…'

'No!' Chu shouted back, his arms were performing dazzling strokes with his blade, arms and heads leapt into the air around him, he was soaked in the blood of his victims. 'We keep going, we push forwards.'

Chu wasn't going to break. They could push him back all they wanted but he would keep fighting. His stamina was endless; Rod had witnessed him performing incredibly strenuous kata's for entire days. He would block, thrust and parry these insane assholes until somehow one of them managed to score a fatal blow or he butchered every last one of them.

He looked up. Maybe now was the time. He could leap back, snatch up Vanessa and they were out of this.

He turned his head to check her position. She was gone.

'Fuck!' He couldn't risk turning his attention from the assault for too long but checked again just to make sure she had not deconstructed and was simply difficult to see. No. She wasn't behind them.

A sudden surge of bodies moved both him and Chu backwards again. They had lost a lot of ground and were staggering inexorably towards the burning jet.

'No one is coming at us from behind.' Rod thought. 'No attempt to stop us retreating and these guys are endless.' For every robed figure Rod smashed, and Chu carved apart, three more appeared to take their place.

'There must be a thousand of them.'

He was getting tired. He didn't have Chu's Enhanced fortitude, he was a good fighter, he was fast and strong and his skin elastic, he healed most injuries far quicker than any normal man but his powers were limited. If he fought much longer he might not have the energy required to fly.

He stepped backwards over a length of metal, probably a piece of TW6's structure, it had lain in a puddle of burning fuel which had begun to dissipate. It glowed red-hot. Rod lifted it with ease, the heat barely noticed by his resistant gloves and Enhanced skin. He began to swing it, as though it was as light as a broom handle. More bodies crumpled to the floor.

Suddenly the assault stopped. The men in robes began to slowly step backwards over their fallen brothers

'They are retreating!' Chu said, 'we have won!'

Rod wasn't so sure. He waved the bar menacingly towards the cultists. None came forward.

'I don't like it.' he said. Something vibrated against his thigh. His phone.

'*God almighty. Alex!*' In the fear and excitement, he had completely forgotten about the phone, about Velocity speeding around the stadium.

He pulled out the phone and looked at the screen. Half a dozen missed calls and texts showed.

'Chu, keep em peeled.' Rod called to his colleague.

Chu nodded.

Rod hit Call Back. Alex answered almost immediately.

'Rod. Jesus. What the fuck is going on in there?'

'It was a set-up up Al. Listen, are the cops coming?'

'Yeah, there's sirens coming right across the valley. I think I can hear a chopper too. What's the situation?'

'The situation is we are fucked. There's an army of guys in here, weird psycho types in robes. Swan is dead, Phantom Lady is missing, same goes for Hyper-Ton. You have to get to the cops and tell them to bring more people, real firepower man. We need the military.'

'Swans dead?' Alex said.

'Yeah, I saw it. We're all going to be dead soon, something is going down right now.'

'I'll be right there man,' Alex said.

Rod thought he could sense excitement in his voice. 'What? No, no… listen just get to the cops and get them to bring the National Guard, SWAT…'

'Are you fucking kidding? TW5 has a spot, there's an opening. If I can get in on this while the Cameras are rolling I'm a shoe in for the team.'

Rod could scarcely believe what he was hearing. *'There's a spot? Swan is dead so there's a fucking SPOT!'*

'Alex don't be a fucking asshole. A young girl just died, just get the military. Jesus!'

'Hey, fuck you Rod Raynes. I deserve a break OK. You think watching you soak up all that fame and green has been easy huh? Don't you think I deserve something for all the help I've given you. Damn, you would be on the floor of a bar right now if I hadn't spent my fucking time listening to your bullshit.'

Rod felt the energy drain out of his body. He was done. It was over.

'I'm coming in there, don't worry nothing's going to stop me. I'll give B&P a show like they've never seen before.'

The line went dead. Rod let the phone slip from his fingers.

'Captain. What's the situation? Chu asked.

Rod didn't look over to him. Instead he looked ahead, because at that point Vanessa emerged from the crowd of men. The huge fingers of Hyper-ton wrapped around her neck. He towered over her, his normally red and scowling face looked pale and slack. Beside them both were two others who were not dressed in cowls.

One he recognised as the serial rapist, one of the guys they had come for, Dream Machine, the other was wearing some form of ceremonial garb but strikingly different from the drab brown robes of what Rod assumed must be his followers.

'*This must be their priest, their leader.*' Rod thought.

'Hey guys.' Dream Machine flashed a toothy smile from under his oil and soot blackened face.

'Vanessa.' Rod called to her. Hyper-Ton's fingers tightened.

'Steady Captain.' Dream Machine said. 'Don't make me nervous with any chit-chat or sudden super-duper hai karate.'

He flicked a finger towards Hyper-Ton. 'Your buddy is pretty easy to control and I might just squeeze a little too hard.'

Rod looked at Hyper-Ton. He wasn't really there. The loudmouth angry bigot had been replaced with a zombie.

'*Mind Control...*' Rod thought. '*Is this what this guy does, control people?*'

'Look, its Richard... Ricky, isn't it? I think...' Rod started but stopped as Hyper-Ton lifted Vanessa off her feet. Her face contorted as her breath was stopped.

Ricky screamed at Rod '*ITS FUCKING DREAM MACHINE ASSHOLE. DREAM MACHINE.*'

'*Holy shit,*' Rod dropped his metal club and raised his hands, 'Ok man, I'm sorry, sure Dream Machine. Absolutely.'

The other stepped forwards. The one who looked a little like a high priest might although as strange as his garb was he looked no more bizarre than the guys Rod had seen at the Catholic church he had attended as a child.

'Mr Raynes, Mr Wan.' the priest said politely.

'Who the fuck are you?' Rod asked.

'My name is Legion,' the man raised his hand slowly then indicated the growing number of robed men gathering around him, 'for we are many.'

'Right, Ok.' Rod said. 'What do you want?'

He looked at Vanessa, she was clawing uselessly at Hyper's fingers, she was suffocating.

'Dream Machine, if it's you doing that could stop it please?' Rod pointed towards Vanessa.

'Fuck you *Captain Cockhole*.' Ricky replied.

'Please, Dream Machine,' Legion said, 'remember our agreement.'

Ricky scowled. Hyper-Ton's grip relaxed a little and he lowered Vanessa so her feet rested on the floor.

'Thank you.' Legion said, and returned his attention to Rod.

'Mr Raynes you join us today on a very special occasion. Today we reveal our people to the world.'

The hand that had indicated his army pointed to the drone cams above them.

'While our little show has not gone entirely according to plan we have confidence that we have shown the power and resources we have available to us, and now I would like to make an offer to you, as I have done with... Dream Machine here.'

'Oh yeah, what's that then.' Rod asked evenly.

It is very simple Mr Raynes. I want you, Mr Wan and Mr Mitchell,' Legion pointed to Hyper-ton, 'to die. Right where you are standing. In return I will free Miss Peel.'

'Oh, is that all?' Rod asked.

'Ah, no, not entirely. There is another in this building that will be required to join you, but he is very close now. So, I'm sure when your friend Alex arrives, he is being assisted by my brothers and sisters at the moment, he will accommodate that request as I have just enjoyed a very constructive conversation with him.'

'Alex?'

'Yes! Mr Velocity! What a very exciting ability he has. However, it seems his interest in the possibility of being the leader of your little group is even more exciting to him.'

'How the hell did you talk...'

'While ours is a deeply spiritual organisation Mr Raynes we are not at all resistant to the advancement of technology. A cell phone is not the most secure way of conversing with one's secret accomplices.'

Rod looked at Chu.

'No deal.' Chu said firmly.

'Vanessa?' Was all that Rod could offer.

'No.' Chu said flatly, 'She knew the risks. We signed up to take out scum like this, we fight to the last.'

Legion smiled. 'Ah, the resolute Mr Wan. Only you see, thanks to my arrangement with Machine here, should you attempt to take one step closer, Mr Mitchell will have his head blown off by one of my brothers, who is stood behind him with a very powerful shotgun. Our friend Dream Machine will then control *your* mind and you will proceed to use your considerable talents in removing Miss Peel's arms and legs. Obviously, you will also take care of Mr Raynes, who I'm afraid to say doesn't have even close to your prowess in combat.'

'I'll take my chances.' Chu replied.

'No,' Rod said. 'Chu, for God's sake. At least let Vanessa walk away from this, she has a kid, she's young, she has chance at a life after this.'

'Well perhaps.' Legion said, interrupting. 'However what matters right now is that we conclude this quickly, and as you two appear to be in a state of conflict concerning my offer I'm afraid I'm going to have to progress with my alternate option. Dream Machine, if you would.'

Legion gestured at Rod and Chu.

Hyper-Ton threw Vanessa towards them. She landed heavily at Rods feet. Hyper moved a step towards them.

Chu raised his sword as Rod pulled Vanessa to her feet.

'Deconstruct, get out of here.' Rod whispered to her.

'I can't,' she said, her words came in-between gasps, 'he did something to me, I don't know what.'

'Unfortunately, it looks like I will have to take care of Mr Storno separately.' Legion said.

Rod could see that Ricky, the fucking *Dream Machine* found that amusing.

'How you all survived that explosion was testament to your reflexes, bravo, however this time there is nowhere to go. You may all at least die knowing that you served a higher purpose.'

He stepped back.

The Legion followers gathered around him and stepped forward producing assault rifles. At this range Rod knew neither he nor Chu would be able to avoid the hail of shots. They would all be shredded.

'Goodbye. Be thankful that your deaths will give life to our master.' Legion said, and disappeared into the throng.

'Adios fuckers.' Ricky said. 'Enjoy the party.' He gave a jaunty salute to Rod and turned to leave.

Rod's enhanced hearing detected the swarm of rocket fire before he saw the missiles coming towards him. His mind quickly worked through the information he had gleaned.

'*The jet was supposed to kill us all, good guys and bad guys, right here.*' He thought.

Micro-seconds ticked by as he unravelled the complex plot that had been hatched.

'*They blew it. That grinning waste of humanity Dream Machine earned his ticket out by helping them, sold out his buddy.*'

He thought of Alex. '*My buddy sold me out too. Guess both me and Sightmaster are real couple of losers today. Alex will be running in to be 'the guy.' I never thought he wanted it so bad that he would become such a dick. And ten to one Dream Machine is going to suddenly find himself friendless. They will feed him to Alex as part of whatever crazy fucking deal they have made to give him fame in exchange for walking out of here.*'

The roar of the rockets was close now, a few more micro-seconds passed.

'*Vanessa ran. I don't blame her. Hyper? Who knows, maybe he ran and they caught him, maybe that dick head got to him before he could recover from the blast, maybe he was part of it all along, I couldn't give a fuck about him. Chu is lost in his own red world of vengeance. All he wants to do is kill all the bad guys, all the time. Having me around is just like having a spare arm to kill more assholes with.*

I'm truly alone. I wish I could save these guys but honestly, I think I welcome death.'

From the corner of his eye he could see the smoky trail of the rockets.

'*I welcome death because I'd rather be dead than alone in this fucking awful world.*'

Rod closed his eyes. And missed the show.

As Trey moved back towards the jet, rather than making a beeline for the terrific brawl happening ahead, he tried to take a more circuitous route so it looked like he was making for an exit. He wanted to see what would happen.

Once he began moving away from the cleared area of the floor the Legion faithful appeared again. They walked out of the smoke with their knives brandished. As he retreated back towards the path of symbols, what just had to be a circle, they halted and fell back.

'*Total trap,*' Trey thought. '*I'm exactly where they want me to be.*'

He wished he had brought extra clips, rather than just carrying all his guns so he looked the part.

'Style over substance Trey Storno, that's what you have right here,' he said, enjoying berating himself.

Despite the halt of incoming fire and the distance being kept by Legion Trey still moved as low and as quietly as he could. He couldn't explain why but he felt empowered, as though in the last ten minutes he had matured in deed and thought. Was it because he now understood he didn't need Ricky to watch over him? Perhaps it was because his power, the Enhanced ability he had thought so limited had been revealed to be far more than he had ever considered.

'*You are not a victim,*' the voice that lived in his subconscious told him. '*You only ever thought you were.*'

That made sense. He had always been led, had often fallen prey to authoritative and commanding personalities like Ricky. Duped by people who pretended to offer the hand of friendship and protection, when all they were really doing was exploiting his loyalty.

'No more,' he decided, 'I'm going to die here, and that's ok, so long as I die free of my own bullshit.'

He stopped and crouched very low. The fighting had paused. Both sides had retreated. The Wild Five, what was left of them at least, stood just a few yards from the burning skeleton of their jet. In front of them a horde of robed Legion fucks gathered.

Two of the figures were instantly recognisable, Dragons Claw, the super cool samurai and Captain Courage, so-called Protector of the Bay, or Asshole Incarnate as Ricky called him, and he was hauling from the floor one of the girls, he thought it might be Phantom Lady, the one who could walk through walls. Now that was a killer power and she was off the fucking charts hot.

Within the Legion ranks he saw a huge man step forwards, to join them he thought, that had to be Hyper-Ton, strong as Ox and just as dumb. Rumour had it Hyper had been a KKK enforcer, one of Senator Chesters goons, but B&P had washed it out of the press if that was the case.

And there, stood next to some asshat in a wild ceremonial get up was his very own Dream Machine. Ricky was stood with a shit eating grin, clearly loving every minute of this.

'Jesus Christ. He set me up. That motherfucker set me up.'

Trey felt sick. As the realisation of what was happening washed over him he got to his knees and began to breathe hard.

'Motherfucker, motherfucker, motherfucker,' he repeated in gasps. 'The King Sphincter of all Assholes, the mighty Dream Machine has sold both me and the dick heads of The Wild Five to this band of Waco Whackjobs.'

Trey took a breath. 'Remember dude, today we don't die of our own bullshit.'

He looked around. There, lying on the floor in plain view was his rifle.

'I'll be damned.' he thought.

It made sense though, this was near to where he had been blasted off his feet. He scrambled over and picked up the weapon. It still wouldn't help him take out Legion and he didn't care too much for The Wild Five, they looked as though they had their own problems right now anyway, but Ricky...

He stood and lifted the rifle to his shoulder. He peered through the scope and brought Ricky's face into focus.

'I'm going to move this bullet in and out of your body, from your feet up, until it reaches your empty fucking heart.'

Abruptly, Ricky and the strangely dressed Legion guy turned away, moving into the crowd. Trey completely lost them.

'FUCK!'

The Legion members at the front of the line all presented riot shields in front of them forming a wall.

Trey was confused. 'The fuck is this now?'

Then the rockets were launched and his ability captured each one through sheer reflex.

The slow time thing happened. Trey moved with them. He could see himself stood below, with his rifle pointed towards the crowd. There were six rockets. Probably the same type of things as had been launched at TW6 and now they were headed for its former occupants.

'Gonna blow em all to hell,' he thought. 'All bunched up like that the blast from these bad boys can't miss. Boom, all gone.'

The riot shields made sense to him now.

'Those Legion fucks at the front will catch a bad case of being blasted to mulch but they will make sure that Ricky and cross-dressing guy are fine.'

Trey lowered his rifle.

'Not today assholes.' he said, and guided five of the rockets towards the Legion crowd.

'Wild Five, you can still have one of them. After all, I am the bad guy.'

Trey whooped and pumped the air as the rockets struck and produced a terrific series of *Whumpf* sounds.

Bodies and body parts flew up into the air and a new smoke cloud quickly joined that of the jet. Trey moved forward. Scanning the shit-storm for any sign of Ricky and as he neared the burning jet he could see two of the TW5 members.

The Captain and Phantom Lady lay feet apart, he didn't see Dragons Claw until he spotted part of the martial artists fire resistant costume. Chu had been blown into the jet and his exposed skin was already charred. He wasn't moving. It was then Trey saw a strut coming out of his chest. Chu had been speared by it.

A deafening 'CLANK' sounded. Trey looked up. The concussion of this new explosion had worked upon the structure of the open roof, already under stress from years of neglect and now excessive heat from TW6 as its high tech body was eaten away by fire. Pieces fell. That he was stood almost in the middle meant he should be safe from anything coming down but he kept a wary eye.

Phantom Lady was out cold, the Captain too.

'*I should pop you two right now.*' Trey thought. He then shrugged. 'Nah,' he said.

He walked over to the mass of Legion dead. There were bodies as far as he could see but it was clear to him that not all had been victims of the blast.

'Boy, these guys really clocked up a body count.' Trey said with admiration.

He stepped over and through them, some twitched and groaned. The floor was a bumpy carpet of brown robes, exposed white skin and deep red blood. He was looking for Ricky, all he wanted to find was Ricky.

A shout came from behind the advertising aboard ahead

'Hey moron!'

Trey realised he had found his former partner and lifted his rifle towards him.

'I wouldn't do that if I were you man,' Ricky shouted gleefully. 'I know you never miss an all but right now you have shit all over you.'

Ricky wasn't bluffing. Slim red beams of light were revealed in the drifting smoke. Trey looked down at the icon on his chest. Angry red dots bobbed about it.

'*He doesn't know. Arrogant narcissistic asshole has no fucking clue what I can do.*'

'Looks like the guys with the rockets could use a few lessons from you buddy.'

As Ricky talked, and talked and talked like he always did, Trey tried to connect with things around the arena. Nothing came to him, he felt no movement that he could pick up and control as he had done with the bullets and rockets. When the Legion men had come towards him he couldn't feel their knives, he couldn't control them like he could like a bullet the moment it left the barrel of a gun at three hundred miles per second.

'Perhaps that's it, maybe it's the speed,' Trey thought. *'Doesn't have to be super-fast, the rock Ricky threw couldn't have travelled at more than thirty to fifty miles per hour.'*

He had read that a non-Enhanced pitcher could throw a ball as fast as one hundred miles per hour, but Ricky was just an average asshole so his guess had to be a least close.

'Why did you do this Ricky?' Trey said.

'It's Dream Machine douche bag, Dream Mach…'

'Fuck you Ricky Jackson, you lying piece of shit. You set me up.' Trey shook his head and lowered his rifle. The little dots still danced across his chest.

'I did!' Ricky said, his smile broadening. 'And it was so easy too. You're the perfect person to feed to the lions because you can't exist without someone to tell you what to do. You're a zero Trey. A nothing. Even with fucking super powers man, you still couldn't manage to rise above being no more than a loser shooting people from a distance. Hell, any jackass could have managed that.'

To Ricky's surprise Trey laughed at this. It annoyed him. He didn't like to be laughed at.

'What's so funny huh?' Ricky bawled. 'You fucking remedial. You fucking…fuck head.'

Trey laughed harder, 'fucking…. oh shit… fuck head?

'*Shoot assholes, come on shoot.*' Trey urged the snipers to do their thing but still the dots just moved about him. '*What are you waiting for Ricky. Why are you stalling?*'

'You're gonna die Trey. Right there and on TV man. So laugh it up. Just one more prick to arrive at the party and its all over for you.'

'*One more?*' Trey thought. He looked about.

A bloodied hand dropped onto Ricky's shoulder and the Legion priest appeared behind him. He hadn't escaped the blast's as lightly as Ricky. He whispered something into Ricky's ear. Ricky nodded.

'Ok dipshit back up. Closer to the jet, stand inside the circle.'

Trey looked down, '*So, it is a circle. Something tells me they don't want me dead until I'm inside it, all this has been to get me and the Wild Five into this thing.*'

Trey stepped back slowly.

'That's a boy.' Ricky called.

Trey saw the Legion priest disappear into the shadows.

'OK. Now I can boogie. Enjoy watching your soul being…'

Trey stopped listening to Ricky as he gloated. Something else had caught his attention. Something was moving, moving fast enough for Trey to catch it. His vision split into two, he saw Ricky, still talking, but as though he had been reduced to a thousandth of his speed, in the other window he saw the tunnel he had walked down to enter the arena. His view was from that of a person who was running. This person ran *fast*, faster than Trey could have ever thought possible. Legion men lined the tunnel, heads bowed, allowing the man to pass unmolested.

'*Enhanced,*' he thought, '*clearly on Legion's payroll.*'

Suddenly the view changed. He was no longer in the tunnel but speeding through some kind of light show. It was incredible. All around him lights, beams of light appeared to be streaking by. Then he was back. He was now in the arena. It was as though he had slipped through a gap in the tunnel and appeared hundreds of yards further forward.

'*Damn, dude is fast.*' Trey thought. He then focused his power upon the running man. '*Let's see just how fast you can go.*'

Alex felt as though he had been pushed a little as he ran. For a moment he thought he might fall as his legs, while they still pumped furiously didn't seem to be running in time with his speed. He had been about to phase into Null Space, he would reach the centre of the arena in seconds thanks to the folded space time, and take down the man who had been killing B&P employees with the Taser he kept in his utility belt.

Legion had promised him he could join The Wild Five and this would certainly seal it. He would capture the bad guys live on TW5 TV! His excitement had risen so much he grinned like a Cheshire cat as he zoomed towards his destination.

Suddenly, his legs lost all synchronisation, yet he was still moving at incredible speed. He hadn't phased out but he was still accelerating. He wore goggles to protect his eyes and they projected a heads-up display, on it he could see his heart rate, blood pressure and speed. The readout leapt from eighty to three hundred miles per hour in less than three seconds and it didn't stop there. The world became a blur. He took a breath, difficult with the force of the smoky air upon his lungs. It would be his last.

His mind only registered that there was someone in front of him as he came within a few feet. He had no time to shout or to scream. He couldn't move one way or the other to avoid the man in the pastel blue suit. Instead, Alex hit Ricky at four hundred and seventy-five miles per hour.

The force ruptured their bodies. Bones fractured, splintered and exploded outwards. Their organs turned to jelly from the compression of the contact. Although the suit that Alex wore was strong it couldn't hold together against the sheer pressure of his liquefied body and it burst open, splashing him across the arena.

Ricky didn't see what hit him. His final vision was of Trey smiling, with laser dots working to and fro across his chest. The impact sent a shockwave through his body which wrenched his arms and head off. As they flew across the stadium his torso was driven along by the remaining mass of Alex's body into the seating three tiers up.

'Nice.' Trey thought, as he caught each of the sniper's shots as they left their barrels. He allowed them to travel a few yards before turning them around in a tight arc and sending them back into the scope of each of rifle. The bullets exited through the backs of their owner's heads.

He pulled out his Desert Eagles and fired four rounds into the air. They became his personal drones, seeing through them, looking for the remaining Legion members. He caught a few stragglers who were making for a service tunnel. Unfortunately for them someone had closed the entry door and locked it.

Trey guessed the Legion priest had no problem with using his followers or Ricky to cover his escape. He let a single bullet take care of each one of them. The rest he used to look for any further threats, but they appeared to be done. The priest clearly left a skeleton staff behind to finish the last part of his job. Trey let the bullets drop harmlessly to the floor, retrieved his rifle and turned back towards the jet.

As he strode back into the circle he looked at Phantom Lady. She appeared to be alive but out cold. Trey thought she still looked incredibly hot too, considering the soot and blood that covered her.

'*Time to check out the exalted leader,*' he thought. Cradling the rifle in his arms he strolled over to where Rod lay.

'Hey, Captain, you still with us?' Trey shouted.

Rod flinched a little, then turned his head and looked up at the figure standing over him. He looked ominous, almost awe inspiring with the flames of the jet licking at the air behind him.

'I'm with you,' Rod replied slowly.

'Well, good for you Captain. I thought you were out for the remainder. You're a tough son of a bitch.'

'Thanks.' Rod replied, he took a deep breath and let it out slowly.

'So what's the story? Trey asked, as though the two had just met at a ball game. 'Can't move? Spine? Legs?'

'I'm fine I think,' Rod replied. 'May I sit up?'

'Sure. Go ahead.' Trey replied, he took a step backwards.

Rod eased himself up. He did feel a little sore but other than that was convinced he only had the wind knocked out of him and a bang on the head. His Enhanced hearing kicked in as he rose and picked up sirens, close, and at least one helicopter.

'A Rocket landed near us.' Vanessa came to his mind, and he quickly looked over to where she lay. 'God, is she...'

'I think she's OK,' Trey said, he turned his head to take another look at the beauty on the floor, 'she's breathing.'

'Thank God.' Rod said, relief washed over him despite his situation being no less dangerous than when the rocket had landed.

'Sorry about that by the way. I was kind of still mad at you guys so I let you have one.'

Rod raised his eyebrows, 'You did that?'

'Yeah, well, kind of. I didn't fire them at you that was our Legion friends. I sort of guided them, if you follow. If it's any consolation I threw the rest at the Super-Mormons.'

'The Super-Mormo... oh right, I'm with you.' Rod nodded. This kid was super cool. Rod thought that if the guy was any more relaxed about the whole thing he might just take a nap.

'Look son, the cops are coming, there's a chopper too and,' Rod looked up, 'we are on every Pay Per View channel Bartlett and Pearce own across the globe, so you might want to scoot. Unless you still have plans with me of course.'

Trey looked around the arena. 'Ahh, I don't give a shit to be perfectly honest. This has been the most fun I'm ever likely to have.' He looked back to Rod. 'I don't have any plans for you Captain, or hot stuff. What's the point?'

Rod licked his lips. The air was hot and dry and the smoke was stifling.

'I heard shouting I think, before I came around,' he said, the memory was distorted, 'an argument or something.'

'Uh huh,' Trey nodded 'that was a guy I knew. I think he ran into a friend of yours, well... vice versa.'

'Right, that must have been Alex. He finally got his moment in the spotlight I guess. Did he arrest your friend?'

'I dunno, they took off.' Trey replied.

Rod grunted. 'Makes sense. Wouldn't want me stealing his glory.'

Trey smiled. The Captain was all right. They were both fucked, just in different ways. For the first time in a long time he felt he was on common ground with someone. Dude was polite too.

He had been waiting for the Captain to make a sudden move, to whip out a knife or produce a gun or at least *something*. Instead the old guy just seemed happy to chit-chat.

'This must all be a bit of a mess for you Captain? I imagine you're gonna catch some heat.'

Rod held up a hand, 'Please don't... don't call me Captain. It's Rod. Rodney Raynes if you want to be a bitch about it.'

Trey smiled. 'Heh, OK Rod, sure. I guess if we are going to be using first names I'm Trey, Trey Storno.'

'Yeah, I know. We actually came looking for you. The Sightmaster, right?'

Trey stopped smiling. 'Nah. Fuck that. I'm Trey Storno, that's enough I think.' He nodded. 'Yeah, that's enough.'

'Storno, it's a pretty cool name,' Rod said, 'if you don't mind me saying. Maybe you could use that in future. Hell, you're on TV now kid so a secret identity is kind of moot.'

'Wouldn't that be something Rod? Sadly, there's no way I'm getting out of this place alive. I've got a talent, I've been working it all out, but there's going to be a limit, there always is with these things. Come at me fast and I can handle myself, stroll up and bop me on the nose and I'm fucked.'

Rod said nothing, he wasn't sure what the young man meant about his talent but it was clear that he was quite prepared for this to be his last day on earth.

'*How ironic*,' Rod thought, that he felt the same way.

'Trey, can I ask you a question?' Rod said after a few moments of silence had passed.

'Go for it.' Trey said.

'Would you consider taking on a sidekick?'

'The fuck are you saying?' Trey said, wondering if he had misheard.

'I mean it. I know I'm old and miserable but I've tried it on this side of the fence and I... I don't know, I fancy giving it a shot from your side.'

'You're fucking with me Rod. I know you are.'

'No sir.' Rod shook his head. 'That's not my style, not at all. Look, I don't think I could hurt innocent people Trey and don't think it's right that you should either, but right now what I want more than anything in the world is a friend, a real honest to goodness friend. And after that, well, I want to hurt Bartlett and Pearce, and I mean seriously hurt them. Financially, physically, everything that goes with that.'

An image of Eddie Banes with his cell phone sticking out of his forehead flashed through Rod's mind.

'You are a hell of a resourceful guy and, bar the wanton murder of B&P employees, I don't actually know that you've done anything particularly nasty. I don't know what you would call a couple of bad guys that beat on other bad guys but that's what I'm offering. That and I've some good intel on a lot of B&P's money operations. You've got the ranged stuff covered and I'm pretty good toe to toe. Storno and Raynes. What d'ya say?'

'Storno and Raynes.' Trey repeated. He considered this for a moment, looking across the stadium, then looked back to Rod. 'No. Sorry Rod, that doesn't work for me.'

Rod nodded, 'Ah well, I have these fancies, it's just my nature.

'Raynes and Storno,' Trey said and grinned. 'It has a better ring to it don't you think?'

Rod laughed, his mood was odd, he felt happy. He nodded and stood. Trey rose with him.

'Rod Raynes and Trey Storno, partners.' Rod said and offered Trey his hand. Trey took it and they shook.

'So what happens now partner?' Trey said as their hands dropped. 'We can go out guns and biceps blazing or burn to death inside this shit hole I suppose.'

118

'Actually, I have another option available to us. Do you think you can keep a hold of Phantom Lady for about five minutes? And I mean a tight hold.'

'Man, I would not let that lady out of my arms if my ass was on fire.' Trey replied.

'Good.' Rod said, and looked up at the open roof of the stadium, 'because it very well may be.'

'There! Look at him. Jesus what's he doing.'

Nils pointed at the screen. The creature had begun to vibrate, his hands had tightened again and his head lifted showing rolled back eyes.

'Rockets just took more of them out I think.' Carver said, keeping his attention on the events on the monitor as they unfolded. 'It's a bloodbath in there.'

'The Wild Five?' Nils asked.

'Yes, kind of. Both sides got hit. In fact, the majority of the fire went into the other guys. Blew them all to hell.'

Nils looked at him, 'Was anyone inside that circle?'

'Yes, all of the remaining Five members.' Carver replied.

'It's connected!' Nils said excitedly, 'It has to be. That circle is the key to all this.'

'What do you mean?' Carver asked, as he watched a single figure, a rifle slung casually over his shoulder, emerge from the smoke and walk amongst the dead. Something had happened off to the side, where he had come from, but there was no coverage to see what.

'When someone dies inside that circle, this thing...' Nils jabbed at the monitor, 'it reacts.'

Nils didn't like where his thoughts were taking him but he was compelled to obey his intellect. He swung around in his chair to face Carver.

'In Arabic legend there was a creature called a Ghoul, it was a spirit, a monster, the things the nomadic peoples call djinn. They ate the dead, fed on their souls.'

'You think it's a djinn? Carver asked, far to calmly for Nil's liking.

'Not as such. I'm saying its feeding on the Enhanced who died inside that circle. Doctor Nevatte said that it looked like the symbols represented sacrifice. So, ask yourself this, sacrifice to what?'

'Coincidence?' Carver asked, he had to be devil's advocate no matter how plausible the professor's theory sounded.

'Once? Sure, I'll give you that. But every fucking time there has been a death inside that particular area? Not a chance. This isn't Enhanced ability at work Commander, this is the supernatural and it... what the fuck is happening now?'

Carver realised Nils was looking at the main monitor. He turned back to it.

The guy with the rifle, who had strolled into view, seemingly chatted with Raynes and was now gathering up Phantom Lady in his arms. Then the legendary Captain Courage walked behind them and in turn wrapped his arms around them both.

'What the fuck?' Carver mouthed.

Nils jaw went slack as Captain Courage lifted into the air, and flew towards the open roof with his passengers held tightly.

'Is Captain Courage running off? With the bad guy and the romantic interest? Nils said, amused.

'Perhaps he's just getting them to safety. He'll arrest the guy when he lands.' Carver said, barely believing the words had left his mouth.

'That guy was covered in weapons, he had a rifle across his back. I really don't think he's going to be arrested.' Nils replied.

'No. Me either.' Carver said. 'Just when I think we have reached maximum weirdness these Enhanced move the goal posts.'

Nils had no argument with that. Furthermore, this was no longer his game. His domain was science. Not Ouija boards and Chucky dolls. He was out.

'Commander I think that you need to look further afield than myself for this project, clearly we have stepped far beyond the… '

'Can it Nils. You are on a three year contract and you are down here with me until its done.'

Carver stood. He pointed at the monitor. 'I want a copy of that analysed tonight, I want every frame studied until your people have bleeding eyes. I want full biometrics on that thing in there, your *Ghoul*. If you are right then what we just witnessed were its followers, its *flock*. I need to know who and what they are and why they have gone public.'

Nils sat silently. Soaking up the orders with every intention of ignoring them completely.

'And we need the Witch. Get her here. I don't care what you have to offer her but we need her help.'

Nils blinked. 'Are you serious? The sole reason that thing is sat in there is because you double-crossed her. She said the next time she saw you she would flay you alive.'

'I'll take that chance.' Carver replied. 'Unlike you Nils my duty comes before my safety.'

Carver marched to the door and opened it, he looked back to Nils. 'None of your complaints or bullshit Nils, get this done, and quickly.'

'Yes Commander,' Nils said, with the same enthusiasm he had for cleaning his ears.

As soon as Carver closed the door behind him Nils reached for his pad.

He had an out.

———

122

Smart guys never walked into a place they couldn't, if push came to shove, get out of. He wouldn't be able to surface for a long time, but he had enough cash squirreled away to keep him going for at least a few years.

'He needs his fucking head examining if he thinks I'm sticking around to look after that bastard thing,' he thought, as he used the back channel he had installed into the facilities mainframe the day he arrived at the facility.

'Demons, witches, ghosts… madness, fuck all that,' he thought as he tapped in a twenty-eight digit password.

This done he moved to his desk and pulled open a drawer. Inside it he had fashioned a very convincing false bottom. He applied pressure to the opposite corners and the base panel popped up. Nils slid out an envelope.

'Vacation time,' he smiled, *'clean white sand and blue…'*

As he slipped the envelope inside his jacket he heard a popping noise behind him. A smell, not unlike that of smouldering plastic drifted into his nose. He rolled his eyes and sighed.

He turned, and was entirely unsurprised to see a beautiful, raven-haired woman standing in his study. At her feet, a circle with exotic symbols was fading from view as though its opacity was being dialled to zero. She was clothed in a long cloak and the dark locks of her hair tumbled over her shoulders, her eyes were green and at close distance appeared to draw you into them. Nils had spent a lifetime trying to avoid such distractions from this woman with spectacular failure.

'Hello Catherine,' Nils said. 'I don't suppose you are here because you have bought me an early birthday present or something, are you?'

'Dad. I need to speak to Commander Carver right away,' the Witch said.

'Well... that's super,' Nils replied.

About the Author

Eddie Skelson is the author of the Crowley series, a novel, Winter Falls and short story collection The Whitby Horror and Other Tales. He has also written three books of the series The Township Chronicles and is producing a 1920's supernatural thriller title, Abraham Church.

Born and raised in the Midland town of Stoke on Trent Eddie is rapidly gaining recognition for his dark humour and memorable characters. He has also produced numerous comedic scripts and characters via the Facebook platform.

He earned a Master's Degree in Creative Writing from Keele University and is an avid fan of board games which he has no room for.

You can discover more information on Eddie Skelson via his Facebook page, Website (when he can be arsed to update it) and Amazon.

www.facebook.com/ eddie.skelson.writer

http://www.amazon.co.uk/Eddie-Skelson/e/B00VB8JH5Y

Did you enjoy this story?

Gaining recognition for any kind of art is a tough job. One of the ways you can help to promote independent authors is to leave a rating on Amazon and/or a review on Goodreads. Why not take a moment to deliver your rating? You don't have to leave any comments but if you do you might be helping future readers find their way to this authors work.

Thank you for taking a chance on this little piece of writing and in advance for your rating or review

Eddie Skelson

www.ingramcontent.com/pod-product-compliance
Lightning Source LLC
Chambersburg PA
CBHW020621120726
47905CB00003B/880